Thank m..

MW01205126

AMBER

CANDACE CONRAD

AMBER

iUniverse books may be ordered through booksellers or by contacting:

iUniverse
1663 Liberty Drive
Bloomington, IN 47403
www.iuniverse.com
844-349-9409

ISBN: 978-1-6632-0579-7 (sc)
ISBN: 978-1-6632-0580-3 (e)

Library of Congress Control Number: 2020913646

Print information available on the last page.

iUniverse rev. date: 08/20/2020

CONTENTS

PROLOGUE

When Ashlyn Weather was in fourth grade, she met Joey Corlow. They instantly became best friends, and they (eventually) started dating and fell in love. When they were in tenth grade, Joey felt that Ashlyn was the love of his life. When he proposed in September of their eleventh-grade year, she said yes. They moved in together and decided they didn't want to wait to marry, so they dropped out of school and married in April.

CHAPTER 1
THE FAMILY

I n early April, Ashlyn Weather and Joey Corlow got married.
Three months later, they had their first baby girl, Amber
Rose Corlow. They were so excited to have a little piece of
both of them in another person.

Three years later, they had twins, Madison May and Emily
Claire Corlow. They were thrilled about having twin girls.
However, one month after they were born, their parents started
coming home drunk and high. Ashlyn and Joey didn't care
much about the girls after that. In their heads, if they just
made sure the kids didn't die, they were fine. They didn't cook,
change, or bathe the girls. Amber had gone from being a three-
year-old older sister to being a mom. It was sad, but Amber got
used to it.

They had very little money and used it for a few groceries,
diapers, and formula. Times were hard for Amber and her
younger sisters. Amber was in charge of everything in the
house—the cooking, which only consisted of microwaved meals
and formula for the babies; the cleaning; and most importantly,
watching after her younger sisters, even though she was only
three. When their parents were off work, they would throw an

"adult" party, and the kids would have to go outside, go to the neighbors, or shut themselves in the bedroom for hours at a time.

Their neighbors, the Deras, were like a second family to Amber and her sisters, and they would often visit them. Mrs. Dera would cook and bathe the girls, and Mr. Dera would often play with them (doing the best he could at his advanced age). The kids would often stay the night over there, for they didn't feel welcome at their own home. The Deras knew of Ashlyn and Joey's negligence and feared for the girls, but they didn't want to alert the authorities because the girls would be taken away.

CHAPTER 2
AMBER'S BIRTHDAY

mber's sixth birthday landed on a Saturday; fortunately, Amber's parents were off work that day. *Yay!* Amber thought as she woke. *Mommy and Daddy might take us out to eat.* She quickly got up, dressed, got her sisters up and ready, and patiently waited for her parents to get up. She remembered that her mommy had told her never to knock on their bedroom door.

Her parents finally came out of their room, and Amber saw her opportunity. "Mommy, can we go out to eat?" Amber looked at her mom with hopeful eyes.

"Why would we go out? You know we don't have the money for that." Amber knew that was all her parents would ever say. "Okay, Mommy. I'm going next door."

"Take your sisters with you." Amber's mom shut her bedroom door.

Next door, Mrs. Dera had baked Amber cookies and made her a special birthday cake. After they all had cookies, milk, and cake, they went back home.

Her parents were in the living room when they got back. "Hi, Mommy!" The twins ran up to her.

3

"Hi, girls." Their mom groaned.

"Mommy, what did you get me for my birthday?" Amber asked.

"It's your birthday?" her mom questioned, seeming confused.

"Yes. I'm turning six," Amber assured her.

"Oh, happy birthday. Now go to your sisters' room or go back to the neighbors'. I don't care which, but take your sisters with you and don't bother us. We're having a party that we have to get prepared for."

"Okay." Amber hoped it was a birthday party.

Amber decided to go to her sisters' room. She played with the little baby doll her mom had bought for her. She heard her parents go into the living room, call their friends, and tell them that there was going to be a party and they'd have to bring their own "stuff." When Amber realized that it wasn't a birthday party for her, she wanted to leave, but her parents told her to stay in the room.

After a little while, she heard the doorbell; it was Mr. Sarajo, her parents' "party buddy." Mr. Sarajo came in and started smoking. Amber immediately took caution and shut her door so she and her sisters wouldn't smell the horrible fumes. She was heading back to play when all of a sudden she fell face-first onto the floor.

"Am, are you all right?" one of the twins asked.

"Sissy?" the other said as they nudged her.

They both rushed into the living room to tell their parents, but they thought the girls were just playing around. Madison ran next door to tell the Deras what had happened, but Emily gave up on trying to tell their parents and called 911 from their parents' room. "Hello, nine-one-one? My sister fell and won't get up. Please come help."

"Mrs. Dera," Madison panted when she arrived at the neighbor's house, "Am fell and won't get up."

Both of the Deras bolted next door with Madison. They too thought the twins were playing, but they wanted make sure everything was okay. When they got there, they ran to the bedroom to find Amber lying on her stomach on the floor of the bedroom. Mr. Dera wasted no time; he quickly picked her up and brought her in the living room, where Mrs. Dera then performed CPR.

Amber's parents finally believed their girls and went over to the phone. "Mommy, I already called nine-one-one," Emily said. The ambulance, police, and fire department showed up.

Mr. Dera ran outside with Amber in his arms and told them to take her to the hospital as soon as possible. The EMTs put her on a stretcher and sped away. The Deras took the twins and followed the ambulance to the hospital. Amber was rushed to the emergency room, still unconscious.

CHAPTER 3

AMBER WAKES UP

An hour later, the police were investigating. "What exactly happened?" asked Officer Grant.

"I don't know, Officer. My husband and I were at home, and before we knew it, Madison was at our house, banging on our front door, telling us that Amber had fallen and wouldn't get up. When we got to her house, she was passed out in her sisters' bedroom on the floor," Mrs. Dera sobbed.

"Who is Miss Madison?"

"Her little sister, sir. She's three."

"May I speak with her?"

"Right this way," Mrs. Dera said as she got up and went over to the twins. "Maddie, sweetie, Officer Grant wants to talk to you. I'll be right over there if you need anything." She took Emily over to another part of the waiting room.

"Hi there. I'm Officer Grant. May I talk to you?"

"Okay," Madison said, her eyes red from crying.

"No need to be scared, Madison. You did the right thing and should feel very proud of yourself," he said, giving her a little hug and sitting next to her.

While Officer Grant was talking with Madison, Amber

awoke. Officer Grant, Mr. Dera, Mrs. Dera, Emily, and Madison dashed in the room; their parents weren't at the hospital yet.

"Amber? Sweetie, can you hear us?" Mrs. Dera asked, sitting by her bed.

"Sissy?" Madison and Emily asked.

No response.

"Amber? Amber, sweetheart, answer me, please," Mrs. Dera pleaded. "Please!" Her sisters were also pleading.

"Hmm?" Amber groaned, her eyes flickering open.

"Oh, thank goodness," Mrs. Dera said with a tone of relief.

"Wh-what happened? Where am I? What's this?" Amber looked around, tearing up and tugging at her IV.

"I'm not sure, baby girl," Mrs. Dera said as she fixed Amber's IV. "Maddie, do you know what happened?"

"No, all I 'member is that Mommy and Daddy were throwing a party and sissy shut the door," Madison replied.

"Oh, so your mommy and daddy were throwing a party? Was it a birthday party?" Mrs. Dera asked.

"No. It was another *adult* party. Mr. S came over and they started talking loud and smoking," Madison explained.

"Wait, so these girls have been living in that house for six years?" Officer Grant asked, listening to their conversation.

"Well, most of their lives, yes, but they spend the night with us some nights and come over during the day when their parents are at work," Mrs. Dera said, and Mr. Dera nodded in agreement.

Emily and Madison could see that Officer Grant was writing something in his book, but they couldn't figure out what it was. Mr. and Mrs. Dera must have known, for they looked worried.

"Will you all come with me, please?" Officer Grant asked.

"Of course, Officer."

She turned to Amber. "Sweetie, I want you to get some rest.

You're safe now," Mrs. Dera assured her. "If you need anything, press that little red button there on the side of your bed." She kissed Amber's cheek. Mr. Dera did the same.

"Okay. Good night. Love you." Amber said, struggling to breathe.

"Love you too, sweetie," Mrs. Dera said.

They all left her room to talk more about what had happened. When they were out of the room, Officer Grant asked for Amber's address and asked about the girls' health throughout the years. Mr. Dera wrote the address down for him as Mrs. Dera told him that the girls hadn't really been sick.

CHAPTER 4

THE TEST RESULTS

A mber's parents finally showed up two hours later. Due to their parents' negligence, the police wouldn't let the parents in Amber's room until they investigated further. The doctor had run some tests on Amber. It took three long hours before the test results came back. Amber was asleep the entire time. When the tests came back, the news wasn't good.

"Mr. and Mrs. Corlow?" Dr. Justin said.

"Yes?" Mrs. Corlow responded.

"I'm sorry to tell you this, but Amber has been exposed to secondhand smoke."

"Oh, is that it? I mean, just the smoke?" Mrs. Corlow asked, chuckling a little.

"Yes, but this is no laughing matter, Mrs. Corlow. I'm afraid she's been exposed to way too much of it. If your other daughters hadn't been there and acted when they did, Amber could've easily died."

"It was that serious?" Mr. Dera butted in.

"Yes. Sad but true. See, Amber is only six and hasn't fully grown and developed yet. So even if it was just a little bit, it could have easily killed her."

"Oh my God! Ashlyn, didn't you hear Amber when she hit the floor?" Mrs. Dera asked, facing Mrs. Corlow.

"Well, no. Joey and I were on the phone, and I thought she just dropped her doll or something." Ashlyn looked worried now.

"That's not what Madison and Emily said."

"Oh, really? And what exactly did they tell you?" she asked, staring at Emily and Madison angrily.

"They told me that you didn't believe them. They told me you were getting ready for a party."

"No, I didn't believe them. They're only three; I thought they were just playing hospital or doctor. Certainly you didn't think they were telling the truth."

"I hoped not. I just wanted to be sure."

"Excuse me, but I must go check on Amber," Dr. Justin said as he headed toward Amber's room.

"No problem, Doctor," said Mrs. Dera. When the doctor was out of sight, Mr. and Mrs. Dera shot daggers at the Corlows for their negligence.

"Ashlyn, what the heck is wrong with you? Your daughter could have died!" Mrs. Dera exclaimed.

"And you, Joey, are supposed to be a responsible father!" Mr. Dera shouted.

"I'm sorry. I thought Amber had just dropped her doll," Mrs. Corlow said, finally showing some emotion and tearing up.

"Did you ever think it could be something else? You two shouldn't even be drinking or smoking around kids in an enclosed area, let alone be throwing that kind of party!" Mrs. Dera was extremely annoyed with them at this point.

Officer Grant spoke up. "Mrs. Corlow, were you and your husband throwing a party when this happened, maybe smoking or drinking?" He stared at Mrs. Corlow.

"Well, we … um … no, Mrs. Dera was just talking about a tea party we were having with the kids."

"Oh, please," Mrs. Dera said. "You two barely had enough money to buy Amber a doll, let alone tea."

"Mrs. Corlow, is this true?" Officer Grant asked.

"No, it isn't. I bought Amber a baby doll, the twins a crib, and I buy food and diapers."

"Officer, may I say something?" Mrs. Dera asked.

"Go right ahead."

"Ashlyn and Joey barely have any money; I cook for Amber and her sisters, food that my husband and I buy and provide. Ashlyn and Joey 'work' from seven in the morning to seven at night, doing God knows what, so Amber is left to care for her sisters for twelve hours a day," Mrs. Dera said angrily. "Amber comes to our house for help. They even forgot Amber's birthday today!"

"Okay. Ma'am, I'm going to need you to go sit over there, please, and stay calm. Mrs. Corlow," Officer Grant said, now looking at Mrs. Corlow, "who pays for your house and bills?"

"We do, Officer, me and my husband," Mrs. Corlow said nervously.

"What do you and your husband do?"

"I'm a waitress at the burger place downtown. I also work part-time at a pizza place, and my husband works in construction."

"Do you have the numbers for these places? And what do each of the schedules look like?"

"Yes, sir. Here are the numbers to the places." She wrote them down on a piece of paper she tore out of a notebook in her purse. "I work from eight to twelve at the pizza place and one to six at Burger Palace. My husband's schedule varies from week to week, but it's mainly nine to six." Ashlyn looked at Joey, who nodded his head.

"Fine, but I'm going to call these places, make sure your stories check out. Mrs. Dera, do you have anything else to say?"

"Yes, I do." Mrs. Dera made her way back over to where they were.

"You may proceed."

"Thank you, Officer. Ashlyn is lying. She doesn't pay for her kids; Mr. Dera and I do—or try to as much as we can. We paid for Emily and Madison's crib. We thought they had another one, but apparently not, and we've bought all of them a couple of toys. Ashlyn did buy Amber a baby doll for her second birthday, but the twins didn't get anything for birthdays or when they were born. I make Amber and her sisters cake and cookies for all their birthdays. I even bathe them because Ashlyn doesn't. They spend all their money on drugs. They didn't even put Amber in school because they claimed to never have enough time or money."

"Mrs. Corlow, is any of what Mrs. Dera telling me true?"

"No, it's not true ... Joey, please tell them." She was now begging her husband to take over.

"Mrs. Corlow, I have a few policemen at your house right now investigating. If what Mrs. Dera tells me is true, you and your husband will likely lose custody of not one but all three of your daughters, and you may go to prison for child neglect and endangerment, along with the possession of drugs."

Just then, Officer Grant's phone rang. He answered it.

"Officer Grant, Officer Truse here. We are at the Corlow residence. We've found several opened prescribed medications, open cigarette packages, ashtrays, food and trash everywhere, and open cases of beer on the floor."

"How about in the rooms?" Officer Grant asked.

"There are only two bedrooms, sir. The kids' room is small, with a small window, one crib, a baby doll, a chair, and a little wooden table. The closet seems to have a few small toys and some clothes. The master bedroom is big, with a king-size bed, dresser, TV, and two nightstands with a lot of open beer bottles, more cigarette packages, and more drugs, prescribed to them as well as other people."

"Be sure to search all the dressers, drawers, anywhere you can get to. Make sure you get all of it out of that house. In addition, call Sheriff Ziree and update him. He knows where I am if he has questions," said Officer Grant. He ended the call and turned to the children's mother.

"Mrs. Corlow, Officer Truse is one of our most trusted cops. Is what he tells me true? Do you have drugs located throughout your house where your children can get to them?"

"Well, yes, Officer, we do have drugs for medical use. But my husband and I only take drugs when we need to. We wouldn't intentionally leave them out. That's crazy. We had to rush to the hospital."

"We were waiting on you for two hours," Mrs. Dera said under her breath, rolling her eyes.

"Mrs. Dera," one of the twins said, "do you have two dollars?"

"What do you need it for?" Mrs. Dera asked with a smile.

"We're hungry. Mommy didn't feed us yet."

"Of course, sweethearts. Let me walk over there with you."

As Mrs. Dera went to the vending machines with Madison and Emily, Officer Grant handcuffed a sobbing Mr. and Mrs. Corlow.

Three days later, Amber was allowed to leave the hospital. Officer Grant came back to the hospital and greeted her, and while Mr. and Mrs. Dera were filling out the paperwork, he told her that she and her sisters would have to stay with Mr. and Mrs. Dera for a little while. Amber was confused but agreed, and the girls left with their neighbors.

Amber didn't know what had happened while she was in the hospital, but Mr. Dera said he would have to go to the police station and give her parents an earful.

"Why are we taking Mr. Dera to the police station? Where're Mommy and Daddy?" Amber had so many questions.

"Sweetheart, do you know why you and your sisters have to stay with me and Mr. Dera?" Mrs. Dera asked.

"Is it because Mommy and Daddy want us to have a sleepover?" Amber asked, smiling.

"Kind of, sweetie, like a long sleepover. I'll explain everything when we get to my house."

CHAPTER 5
THE TALK

After they dropped Mr. Dera off at the police station, they arrived at Mr. and Mrs. Dera's house. Mrs. Dera was getting worried about Amber and how well she would take the news about her parents. "Let's go inside and talk," Mrs. Dera said to Amber.

They went inside and sat on the couch while Madison and Emily sat on the floor and watched TV. "You, Madison, and Emily will have to come live with Mr. Dera and me for a little while."

"Why? Are Mommy and Daddy going to jail?" Amber was worried and confused.

"Sweetheart, your mommy and daddy love you so much," she said, trying to calm Amber's nerves. "It's just that, well, they drink and smoke too much."

"So just make them stop."

"I'm afraid it's not that easy, baby."

"But why not? Mommy and Daddy promised nothing bad was going to happen."

"I know, but, Amber, sometimes people make promises they can't keep. It's sad, I know, and people may cry, but can you promise me you'll be a big and strong girl for your sisters? And for Mr. Dera and me?"

"I guess so. How long are Mommy and Daddy going to be away?"

"I wish I knew, baby girl. Mr. Dera will be back in a little while. Oh, here he comes now."

When Amber saw Mr. Dera, she ran for the front screen door of the old house. "Mr. Dera! Mr. Dera! What did Mommy and Daddy say? Did they say when they are coming back? Did they say they loved me? Please tell—" Mr. Dera laughed, interrupting Amber. "Your mommy and daddy said they love you and are very sorry for what happened."

"It's okay," Amber said. "I'm all right now. And now we have you and Mrs. Dera to take care of us while Mommy and Daddy are away. I'll be fine. How are they?"

"Amber, please let him take a breath," Mrs. Dera said.

"I'm sorry, Mr. Dera."

"It's okay. I know you miss your mommy and daddy," he said.

They heard a knock on the door. It was Officer Grant with Sheriff Ziree. "Hello, Mr. and Mrs. Dera. Girls. This is Sheriff Ziree. He's going to give you the news of whether the girls will live here or go to a foster center."

"Yes, Officers. Come on in. Please take a seat."

"Thank you."

While Mrs. Dera went to make tea, she asked Amber and her sisters to go to their playroom and play.

"Thank you so much for coming, Officers," Mr. Dera said as he shook their hands.

"You're very welcome, sir," said Sheriff Ziree. "Now, let's get down to business. Amber and her sisters have been exposed to secondhand smoke and have been around other drugs for quite some time now, correct?"

"Yes, sir. They've dealt with it pretty much their whole lives. Well, except when they come over here or are outside."

"And nobody bothered to call the authorities, correct?"

"Only because Ashlyn and Joey begged us not to. They said that they had it all under control and that the children weren't in any danger. We've called the police a few times, but somehow they managed to get away with it."

"Did you believe they could handle it? Did you think they could've hurt or injured these girls in any way?"

"I thought everything was fine. I knew them when they first moved in and had Amber. They were such good parents and wanted her to have everything. They didn't smoke or drink at that time, at least that I saw. All the smoking, drinking, and partying started after the twins were born. I never wanted to think anything would happen. I've seen Ashlyn come home drunk some nights, but Joey usually came home sober. And on the nights any of them were drunk, Amber and her sisters came over here to spend the night."

"Not calling the cops the minute you found this out is considered illegal."

"But, Sheriff ..." Mr. Dera began.

Sheriff Ziree put his hand up. "However, since Amber and her sisters are happy and healthy here, we will drop this and will allow them to stay with you and your wife. We wouldn't want them to be somewhere where they would possibly get separated," Sheriff Ziree finished.

Just then, Mrs. Dera came in with the tea. "Thank you so much, Sheriff. This means so much to me and my wife," Mr. Dera said with the biggest smile. Mrs. Dera sat down, and while they drank their tea, they all explained to her what had happened.

"Well, we'd best get going," Sheriff Ziree said. He and Officer Grant stood. "Thank you so much, and God bless you," Mrs. Dera said.

"Thank you for the tea. It was delicious. We'll be checking in on the children every couple of days for the next few weeks." The sheriff and officer shook their hands and left.

CHAPTER 6
THE BAD NEWS JUST WON'T STOP

A mber and her sisters loved living with the Deras. Four days after moving in with them, they bought the girls their very own beds. The girls still had to share a room, but it was better than sleeping on the couch. Amber loved it. The sisters had fun and played together all day until they had to go to bed. To them, it was the best home ever; they didn't want anything to change.

Almost nine months had passed, and Amber and her sisters were loving life more than ever. The twins had turned four in that time, and they all started school. They didn't ask about their parents much anymore, which relieved the Deras.

When Mr. Dera became ill, Mrs. Dera spoke to the sheriff and CPS and told them she and her husband were getting too old and weak to raise three little girls. CPS had agreed with them and told them they would find someone.

A few weeks later, a caseworker came over and told Amber

and her sisters that they would have to go live with their aunt Sophie, whom they'd never met. They didn't want to because they loved the Deras, but after Mrs. Dera explained to Amber that they would be happier, Amber agreed, as did her sisters.

Five weeks later, they went to live with their aunt Sophie in Atchison. Sophie was twenty-seven. She was a nice woman who worked at a hospital almost all day, but she still had time to keep up her house and have a decent social life. She wasn't married, but she didn't care. She loved her life and everything about it. She lived in a big house. Actually, it wasn't that big, but to Amber it was, and she got her own room apart from the twins; she wasn't used to that.

When their aunt went to work, they stayed with Mandy, Sophie's best friend. Mandy was like a best friend that the girls had never had. She was twenty-five, always hyper, very skinny, pretty, made friends with everybody, and had a great personality. Amber thought they'd be very happy there.

One night when their aunt was home, they were all gathered in the living room. Their aunt was watching her favorite show, *Wheel of Fortune*, and Amber and her sisters were playing with their toys when they got a call. It was Sheriff Ziree. Amber couldn't believe it. It had been a while since she heard from him.

"Yes, I understand. I'll tell them. Thank you so much for the call," Aunt Sophie said, and then she hung up. "Amber, sweetie, come here." Amber got up and went into her aunt's outstretched arms. "I hate to tell you this, but sweet Mr. Dera died. He had a heart attack. He was such a great person."

"No, no, he didn't, Aunt Soph. He's at home with Mrs. Dera." Amber smiled, but she could see that her aunt was serious and her smile went away. By this time, they both had tears they were trying to hold back.

"Amber, I'm sorry. He died, and Mrs. Dera is in the hospital."
When Amber heard that, she stormed out of the living room and
went straight to her room, crying into her pillow.

"Girls, it's bedtime. Go brush your teeth and go to bed,"
their aunt said. The girls got up and did as they were told.
Sophie went to Amber's room to see if she was all right.

When she reached Amber's room, she found the door
locked. "Amber, I'm so sorry this happened, but if it makes
you feel any better, they were my friends too and I love and
miss them as much as you do. Please open your door."

Amber barely opened her door a crack. "Really? You love
and miss them too?"

"Of course I do. They babysat me when I was little." Her
aunt smiled when she said that.

"Really?"

"Yep. In fact, I was your age when my dad died. I remember
it being the hardest time ever. But, Amber, do you know what
happened?" Amber leaned closer. "It hurt at first, but eventually
I felt better ... and you will too. I know you will. You're so
strong and brave. Don't worry. Go to bed now; we'll talk more
about this tomorrow. I have to go check on your sisters. Good
night."

"Good night, Aunt Sophie," Amber said, no longer crying.

When everybody woke up the next morning, they went to
visit Mrs. Dera in the hospital. Mrs. Dera was awake and eating
her lunch. She was so excited to see them.

"Hi, Mrs. Dera!" Amber and her sisters said as they went
to give her a hug. "Hey, baby girls," Mrs. Dera, returning their
hugs. "What are you doing here?" she asked, looking up and
greeting their aunt.

"Mrs. Dera, Aunt Soph said you were sick. I knew you

weren't. I tried to tell her, but she didn't believe me," Amber said.

"Oh, sweetheart, listen, I am feeling a lot better, but I'm afraid I'm still a little weak."

"Don't worry, Mrs. Dera. Like Aunt Soph said, things will get better," Amber declared, smiling as she looked at her aunt. The girls and their aunt stayed at the hospital for a couple of hours talking to Mrs. Dera before heading back home.

"I told you Mrs. Dera wasn't going to die," Amber said proudly when they pulled into the driveway.

"I'm glad I was wrong and you were right. Here, take your sisters inside. I have to go to work, but Mandy's inside. I want you all to take a bath tonight," her aunt said, still worried about Mrs. Dera.

A few nights later, they received another call from the sheriff. Amber thought it had something to do with Mrs. Dera and how she was faring. Unfortunately, Mrs. Dera had passed away in her sleep.

Amber felt as if her heart had stopped. She went to her room and cried while Mandy got her sisters ready for bed and called Sophie at work.

After hearing the news, Sophie explained to her boss what happened; he allowed her to leave early.

"Amber?" Sophie said when she reached her bedroom door and entered.

"Aunt Soph, what are you doing home?"

"I heard what happened. I'm sorry, baby."

"It's okay. Like you said the other night, it'll get better. It *will* get better, won't it?"

"Sure it will, Amber," Sophie said with a smile, but this wasn't just any smile. This was a smile that said, *It will get better, I promise,* and Amber knew it was true.

"You all right now?" Sophie asked.

"I guess so," Amber replied.

"Okay, it's your bedtime. Good night, baby girl."

"Good night, Aunt Soph."

"Mandy, can I ask of you a favor?" Sophie asked when she entered the living room.

"Yes, Emmy and Maddie are in bed. They had a bath and brushed their pearly whites." Mandy smiled.

"Thank you, Mandy, but what I want to ask of you is very serious." She started crying. "I'm afraid it breaks my heart."

"What is it, Soph?"

When Sophie calmed down, she continued. "Mandy, you know the guy I've been talking to?"

"Yes. Harvey, correct? He's very gentlemanlike."

"Yes. Well, it seems that he drove all the way up to my work at the hospital and proposed to me earlier."

"Oh, congratulations! You must be so excited."

The look in Sophie's eyes said it all; she was not excited—not even a little happy—just scared and sad.

"Hey, are you okay? Would you like me to make you some tea or hot cocoa?"

"No, thanks, Mandy."

Mandy was a little confused, as it was a rare occasion when Sophie passed up cocoa or when she was sad when she was talking about Harvey; she was always excited and energetic. "Mandy, you know you're more than my best friend; you're also my other half who cleans the house and takes care of me, and the girls and I love you."

"I love you and the girls as well. And you're my best friend too." Mandy giggled but couldn't figure out why Soph was acting so weird.

"Mandy, Harvey is, or was, amazing. I said no to him."

Sophie didn't know how to tell Mandy that her boyfriend hated children.

"Oh, sweetie, I'm sorry. I know how much he meant to you." Mandy pulled Sophie into a hug.

"Mandy—" She stopped talking as the phone started ringing. It was Harvey. While Sophie talked to Harvey, Mandy got up to make hot cocoa.

"Yes, Harvey. I'm asking Mandy right now if"—tears started falling down her cheeks—"she can watch over them." She hung up the phone just as Mandy brought her a cup of hot cocoa and a box of tissues.

"Oh, thank you, Mandy."

"You're welcome. What did you mean by asking me to 'watch over them'?" Mandy was worried about the girls. She loved them as if they were her own. "Mandy, I was going to lie to you about why you need to watch the girls, but I can't lie to you. The truth is … Harvey threatened to hurt the girls unless I marry him." She started sobbing.

"What? He can't do that! You need to call the cops. Come here." Mandy put her arms around Sophie and hugged her until her sobs turned to little whimpers.

"I've told him that my nieces are the only family I have here and there's no way I can give them up. Mandy, if you do this for me, I swear I'll owe you big time."

"What is it?"

She took a deep breath and wiped her eyes. "Harvey doesn't like kids. He said he loved them at first, but it turns out he changed his mind. I need to ask you to watch over Amber and her sisters after I get married. I'll still come see them, but without Harvey. You're the only other person I can trust with them."

"I honestly don't know, Soph. I wish I knew, but I'm sorry …
I'm really tired. Can we please finish this tomorrow?"

"Okay, but we will discuss this?"

"Of course."

With that, Mandy said goodbye and went home.

CHAPTER 7

ANSWER

Mandy came over the next morning. The kids were in the kitchen eating breakfast, and Sophie was quietly crying in her room. "Good morning, beauties. Where's Sophie?" Mandy asked, energetic as always.

"I think she's in her room," Amber said.

"Okay," she said, kissing the girls before skipping to Sophie's room.

"Hey, Soph. Good morning," Mandy sang with a big smile on her face.

"What's so good about it?" Sophie groaned.

"Oh, come on, Soph, cheer up."

"Why should I? I have to get rid of my nieces. Not to mention the horrible man I have to marry, whom I thought I loved."

"Hey! I know. What if I tell you some good news?" Mandy said, still smiling her big smile.

"Like what, Mandy?"

"On the car ride home last night, I thought long and hard about it, and I've decided that I'm going to take in Amber, Emily, and Madison."

"Really?" She looked up at Mandy, hopeful.

"Yes. I mean, they're amazing girls who deserve a better life than with some strangers. Besides, I love them like you love hot cocoa."

Sophie chuckled. "Yeah, I do love my hot cocoa, don't I?"

Mandy started laughing. "Yes, you do."

"You are the best friend ever," Soph said as they hugged. "For the next eight months before the wedding, why don't we all have fun? Hey, Amber's birthday's coming up. We should do something special."

"That's why I got five passes to Disney World—for you, me Amber, and her sisters—and they're for one day between the sixteenth and twentieth of July."

"That's amazing! What's today?"

"June twelfth. How about we go the nineteenth?"

"Okay, I'm off today so let me get up and we can eat breakfast and go to ... um ..."

"How about we go bowling just down the street?"

"Bowling it is. Please get the girls ready."

When they reached the bowling center, Mandy went to buy drinks, snacks, and shoes. Sophie and the girls found a table and went to claim it. They ate, bowled, and had an amazing time. Then they went to the park and had more fun. They eventually went home, and the kids went to bed.

When Sophie and Mandy were sure the kids were asleep, they talked more about Harvey. Then they talked about their trip to Disney World. Mandy spent the night, and she and Sophie stayed up until midnight, watching movies in Sophie's room.

The next day, Mandy and Sophie told the kids about their plans to go to Disney World.

"That sounds like fun!" Amber said excitedly. Sophie and

Mandy were glad they could give the kids enjoyment before they had to leave.

Sophie put a calendar on the fridge so they could count down the days until they went to Disney World. She had to go to work that day, so Mandy took the kids back to the park. Sophie didn't get off until eleven, so Mandy spent the night again.

The next day, they went to Pizza Party, a pizza place not too far from Sophie's street. It had an arcade about the size of half a Walmart. Sophie bought the girls tokens. As the girls went to play, Sophie and Mandy sat down.

"Mandy, I have a surprise … but you have to promise not to tell the girls. Let me tell them," Sophie said with a smile.

"Oh, did Harvey change his mind? Is the wedding off?" Mandy asked with a hopeful look.

"No, sadly." Sophie was clearly unhappy.

Mandy's hopeful smile turned into a smile to cheer her up. "Hey now! Remember to be strong for your nieces. Anyway, what's the surprise?" Mandy asked, nearly at the edge of her seat like a little girl.

"I bought a three-day Disney World package," Sophie said.

"But I already told you I bought passes."

"Yeah, you bought us one pass each, but my package gets us three days at Disney World plus five nights at a hotel."

"Oh, that's cool! So we're going to Disney World for five days?"

"No. My package is for three days at Disney World, and yours is for one, which means four days, and then the fifth day can be for us just to relax, go shopping, or whatever."

"OMG, that's so cool."

"I know, right!"

"But wait … How can you afford this?"

"They gave me a bonus since I worked sixteen extra hours this week. Plus, I used some of my savings."

"I guess your having me watch the kids extra was worth it, huh?" Mandy teased.

"Yeah, but as I said, don't mention this to the girls. I want to tell them." After their pizza got to the table, they called the girls over. After they ate, the girls played for a while longer before they left for home. They all ate, played a couple of hours more, and went back home.

The rest of the month before their trip went fast. They went to the movies, the skating rink, the bowling alley, the park, and to visit some of Mandy's and Sophie's friends.

CHAPTER 8

DISNEY WORLD

A couple of days before Amber's birthday, they arrived at their hotel by Disney World. A bus would take them to Disney World and back. They were all very excited. When they got to their room, they unpacked everything.

"This is so cool!" Amber said as she looked around and ran out to the balcony.

"Pretty!" Madison said, running around.

"Look—Mickey!" Emily pointed at a picture of Mickey.

"Yes, it is pretty and cool, and yes, that's Mickey." Sophie laughed. "Which beds do you want? We have to share."

"Um, this one!" Amber jumped on the bed.

After they figured out the sleeping arrangements, Sophie told the girls the news about how long they would be staying. The girls jumped on their aunt, nearly pushing her off the bed. Amber was ecstatic; she had never been this happy.

Sophie checked the time. "Five o'clock. I think we have a little time to go look around and swim some."

"Yay!" everybody shouted.

They went to check out the shops in the lobby and then went for a quick swim. This would be their home for four days.

On the first full day, they went to Epcot. They woke up at seven thirty to get ready to go. They didn't want to wait too late. The girls were so excited that they had barely slept. By eight thirty, the girls were ready, and they decided to watch a little TV before they left. While they watched TV, Sophie sprayed the girls with sunscreen and packed it in her bag. Twenty minutes later, they went down to wait for the bus. The bus arrived at nine and took them to Epcot.

"Whoa, will this take us to Disney World?" Madison asked Sophie.

"Yes, it will, Maddie. The wheels to Disney World go round and round, round and round ..."

The girls shouted and giggled. The ride took about ten minutes. When they arrived at Epcot, they walked around a little bit. Amber wanted to go in every direction, and Sophie was relieved that she'd bought a bracelet safety device to keep Amber close. "Look, it's so pretty!" Amber said as she looked around.

"It's hot too," Emily said.

"And crowded," Madison chipped in.

"Let's go get some drinks and a stroller for you two," Sophie said. Sophie rented a two-person stroller for Emily and Madison and then went and bought some drinks. They walked around, shopped, and rode rides for the rest of the day.

The bus ride home wasn't that bad. Their bus stop was the second one, and they were happy to be back to the hotel after a long day. It was around nine, so they decided to unwind in the room, take baths, and get ready for bed.

They spent the next few days essentially the same way. They walked, strolled, shopped, rode rides, and enjoyed the pool. They also went to a few other Disney World parks. Amber loved her early birthday present.

On their last day there, Sophie slept in. When she woke up, she wanted to relax in the hot tub. She and Mandy went down and sat in the hot tub while the kids swam in the pool. They were outside by themselves so the kids had the whole pool to themselves. They played with the toys that Sophie had gotten them, a beach ball and little pool toys. Sophie moved a water basketball goal closer, and they all played water basketball. They'd been in the water for two hours when Sophie told them it was time to get out.

They went back up to the room, got dressed, and went to see more of the city. They saw many stores and souvenir shops. When they stopped at one of the stores, Sophie told the girls they could each pick out one thing. Amber and Emily each picked a little stuffed Simba, and Madison picked out a stuffed Stitch. When they were through sightseeing, they went back to the hotel.

It was five o'clock, so they went to a restaurant in their hotel. After that, they went back upstairs, bathed, and played until bedtime. They had to get up early to leave, so they all went to bed early.

The next morning, they woke up at seven and were sad to leave, but they were somewhat happy to go back home. Amber and her sisters slept in the car for another hour or so.

Sophie tried not to think about their futures apart, but it was only a matter of time before the girls had to move out of her house and into her best friend's home.

CHAPTER 9
SCHOOL

B eep! Beep! Beep!

"Turn off the alarm!" Amber cried.

"Sorry, sweetness, but you have school and I have work. Now chop-chop. I'll go wake your sisters."

Amber was happy to go to school, but she was also sad because summer was over. She was worried about whether the kids would like her or not. Amber got up, dressed, and went to the kitchen to get breakfast. "What if the kids don't like me?" Amber asked.

Sophie reassured her. "Don't worry about them. Worry about yourself and your sisters. If anything bad happens or if the kids say anything bad, tell the teacher."

Amber and her sisters ate, finished getting ready, and piled into their aunt's car. They drove up to Atchison Elementary School and saw a banner that read HELLO AND WELCOME BACK, STUDENTS! in pretty colors. They parked, and Sophie took the girls into the office to make sure they were all set before she left. "Okay, girls, be on your best behavior and Mandy will pick you up at three right outside the door there."

"All right. Bye, Aunt Soph," Amber said, still nervous about their first day.

Amber had been to school before, when they lived with the Deras, but her sisters hadn't. Amber didn't know how well they would do.

"Hi, my name's Chelsea. What are your names?" a nice brown-haired girl around the age of twelve asked.

"Hi, I'm Amber. And these are my sisters, Madison and Emily."

"Hi there. Great to meet you. You guys must be new here." She smiled. She asked the woman working behind the desk what classes and grades Amber and her sisters were in and showed the twins to their classroom. "Now that you know where your sisters will be, do you feel better?" Chelsea asked Amber.

"Yes, I feel a lot better now. Thank you."

"You're so welcome. Your class is right up here." When they got to Amber's class, the bell rang and Chelsea said she had to go. Everyone piled into the class and sat down. There were about sixteen kids in her class. The teacher walked in dressed in a nice dress. She had lovely brown hair. She seemed nice, and Amber just knew she'd love it there.

After the last bell rang, Amber went down the hall to where her sisters' room was. She found them putting stuff in their backpacks. "Come on—Mandy's waiting on us."

They walked to the front door, and sure enough, she was right where their aunt said she'd be. "How was school?" Mandy asked as the girls climbed into the car.

"It was awesome. I want to come back tomorrow!" Emily chirped.

"Good. What about you, Madison?"

"I love it! Our teacher's super nice, and we played games and had snacks."

"And you, Amber?"

"It was good. I like the class, and my teacher's wonderful. I met a few kids I like."

"That's great. I'm glad you girls like your school."

They decided to go see Sophie at work and have a little snack with her before they went home, where they played outside and watched TV for a little bit before eating dinner. Then it was bath time. They all took baths and got ready for bed just as Mandy finished cleaning.

"Okay, bedtime." Mandy went to the twins' room first and then Amber's, making sure they were all in bed. Once they were all asleep, Mandy relaxed, watching TV and sipping hot tea until Sophie came home.

"Hey, Soph, the girls are all asleep."

"Thanks, Mandy. I'll pay you next week when I get paid. I'm sorry. It's late, and I'm exhausted."

"Oh, that's all right. I'll see you and the girls tomorrow."

The next day, Sophie woke up early, showered, and got the girls up for school. She called the girls into the kitchen for breakfast, but when they walked in, they weren't dressed yet and they looked dead tired. "Morning, girls."

"Morning," they all murmured at once, obviously still half-asleep.

"How was school yesterday? Sorry I couldn't pick you up but duty calls."

"It was good. I'm ready to go back again, but why do we have to wake up so early?" Amber asked.

"Oh," Sophie chuckled, "I don't know. But you need to eat and then go get dressed. Mandy will get you again today."

"Aunt Soph, why do you work so much?"

"Well, I have to pay for this house and the food you eat, and you did like that trip to Disney World, didn't you?"

"Yes."

"Well then, that's why. Now eat and then go get dressed and brush your teeth." They finished eating, got ready, and piled in the car again.

"Bye, girls. Have an amazing day. Love all of you," Sophie said as the kids were getting out of the car.

"Bye, Aunt Soph," they replied simultaneously.

They walked toward the school and were greeted by a mysterious man in a nice suit. "Hello, girls. Going to school?" the man asked.

"Yes, sir. Excuse us," Amber said, grabbing her sisters' hands and trying to walk past the man. "Excuse us," Amber said again.

"Oh, my apologies, dear. I'm looking for Amber, Emily, and Madison Corlow."

"That's us, sir. May I help you?"

"Yes. My name's Harvey. I'm your Aunt Sophie's boyfriend, and I love her very much."

"We love Aunt Sophie too," Amber said with a smile, feeling a little calmer knowing he knew her aunt.

"Well, you see, young lady, I asked her to marry me."

"Ah."

"And she said no because of you three," he said, pretending to be sad.

"Why? We wouldn't care if you and Aunt Sophie got married."

"Well, you three are taking all her time when she should be with me, not to mention that I can't move in with her now."

"Why not?" Amber asked.

"Your aunt says you three have been through so much and she wouldn't want us to get too attached."

The school bell rang, letting them know they had to go. "I'm sorry, sir, but we have to go to class now." Amber grabbed her sisters' hands again.

Before they went inside, he picked them up and was about to make a run for it when a female voice came from behind him. "Harvey? What are you doing here? And why are you holding those children? Unhand them now!" She ran toward him. He didn't let them go but just kept running. The woman called the cops and said that someone was trying to kidnap three small girls. The cops caught him. Harvey let them go, and the cops brought them back to the school.

Amber and her sisters were shaking. They got back to the school and called Sophie right away. They had the girls sit in the office instead of going to class. Sophie arrived and immediately hugged her nieces. Once Sophie saw that they were safe, she gave the okay for them to go to class. She then went into the principal's office to ask the helpful woman who the mysterious man was. Nobody had told her over the phone. Sophie sat down, shaking and sobbing from the thought of almost losing her nieces.

"Hello, Ms. Smith," the nice woman, who was also the principal, said.

"Hi. You can call me Sophie."

"All right. So, Sophie, we usually don't have any type of kidnapping at this school, I'm sure you've heard our school is one of the safest here."

"Yes, ma'am."

"Now, when I looked out of the school window this morning, I saw two little girls talking to this man. I couldn't see his face because he had his back to me, nor did I see the two little girls' faces. I assumed it was a father. He moved a little, and I got a glimpse of Amber and her sisters trying to walk away, which is when I immediately got up."

Sophie, now hysterical, grabbed a tissue.

"Do you know a Harvey Vince?"

Sophie froze. "Har-Harvey Vince? Did he do this?"

"Yes, ma'am. I didn't recognize him at first."

"Oh my God."

"When I walked out, the last thing I heard was Amber saying, 'We have to go to class now,' and that's when Harvey picked all three of them up. I asked him why he had the girls and why he was even at the school. I've known Harvey from back when we went to school together, and I know he doesn't like children. Never has. So why would he come up to the school and pick up three little girls? When I asked him about it, he dashed off, carrying the girls. I was able to call the police, and they came immediately, catching him and bringing the girls back. How do you know Harvey, Sophie?"

"He's my … uh … fiancé."

"Fiancé, huh? Well, I take it he doesn't like the fact that your nieces live with you then?"

"No, ma'am … He said if I didn't marry him, he would hurt them. And if I did, he would let them live, just not with us."

"Why haven't you called the police yet?"

"He said no police or he would hurt them, me, and my best friend. Please, Principal Taylor, don't tell anybody. I have it under control. Harvey said the girls could live with me until the wedding, and then they will go to my best friend, Mandy. Mandy's the girl who picked them up yesterday."

"Sophie, we cannot allow this sort of stuff to happen at this school. Please talk to Harvey about it. If he pulls this again, the girls will have to be suspended. I'm sorry, but we can't allow this around the other children."

"I completely understand, Principal Taylor. I'll talk to Harvey about it."

"Okay, be sure you do. Harvey went with the police earlier, so you might want to try going to the police station if you can't reach his phone. The girls are safe here as long as nothing like that ever happens. Just make sure that when you drop the girls off, you watch them go into the building. We'll also make sure we have more teachers present in the mornings."

"Thank you so much, Principal Taylor. You saved my girls," Sophie said as she stood up and turned to leave.

"I'll notify their teachers about this situation. Have a good day, Sophie."

CHAPTER 10

BYE, ATCHISON

A s soon as she left, Sophie headed straight to the police station to meet with the man who'd turned her world upside down for the worse.

"Hello, darling," Harvey said, a big smile on his face when he saw her walk in.

"Don't 'Hello, darling' me, punk!" Sophie snapped back.

"Whoa, ouch. I hope you don't plan on calling me names after we're married," he smirked.

"Oh, I'll call you way worse names than that."

"Hi. Excuse me. Who are you?" the officer on duty asked.

"Hi. I'm Sophie Smith, his ... fiancée," she said with a fake smile. "Um, how long is he going away for? Because, you know, I'll miss him terribly," she lied.

"I'm afraid I can't give you that information, ma'am."

"Okay, thank you. Can you give us some time alone, please?"

"Sure, ma'am. I will put you two in this room right over here. He has to remain handcuffed though."

"Oh, that's fine. We won't do anything, just talk."

Once the officer got them situated in the room and left,

Sophie went ballistic. "All right, Mr. Vince, I'm going to ask you this once: why would you try to kidnap my nieces?" She started shooting daggers at him, but that didn't seem to have any effect on him at all.

"Oh, come on, baby. Do you think I was really going to hurt the girls? I mean, they're, what, six and three? Why would I want to harm them?" He tried to seem innocent since he assumed the cops were listening in.

"They're seven and four. I know what you're doing. You think the cops are listening in because we're in an interrogation room. But don't think I'll let you get away with this, Harvey Vince."

"Oh, you're sexy when you're feisty." He smirked at her again, which caused her to punch him squarely in the mouth.

"If you smirk at me one more time, you won't ever smirk again. If you come at my nieces one more time, not even the police will know where to find you." By now, she was in his face, with her back to the camera, and talking low but angrily so if the police were listening, hopefully they couldn't hear her.

"Anyway, love, I've got to go. Work's calling me, but I will come by later, okay?" she said in a cheerful voice as she got up, grabbed her purse, and turned to leave.

"Ugh! I'm so pissed off!" Sophie said as she and Mandy were sitting in the living room, the girls already in bed for the night.

"What is it?"

The girls hadn't told Mandy anything in fear of getting in trouble, and their principal had only said, "The girls had a rough and tiring morning. Just make sure they get home and to bed safely and get a good night's sleep."

"Mandy, didn't the girls tell you what happened this morning?"

"No, I asked them, and they just said they didn't eat a good breakfast and they were really tired."

"Mandy, someone attempted to kidnap them at school this morning."

"*What!*" Mandy screamed.

"Shhh ... Mandy, don't wake them up. I know it's strange and out-of-the-blue random. Yes, someone attempted to, but it obviously wasn't successful. Luckily, the principal of the school called the cops and saved them."

"Well, thank God. Do they know who it was? Do you know?"

"Yeah, I do. And trust me, I had a few choice words for him at the police station."

"Him?"

"Mandy ... it was Harvey."

"That son of a bitch! I should rip off his man parts or—"

"Mandy?"

"What?

"Calm down. I know you want to get back at him. I do too. But he's going to be going to prison. I'm not sure for how long though."

"I hope he gets raped in that prison," Mandy spat as she rolled her eyes. They both burst out laughing at that thought.

The next morning, the girls woke up and got ready for school. Sophie and Mandy were already in the kitchen making them breakfast.

"Hey, Mandy. What are you doing here?" Amber asked. She was in a much better mood than the morning before.

"I spent the night and told Sophie I would ride to school

with you, and since she's off today, I'll spend the day with her."
Mandy and Sophie smiled.

They didn't want to tell the girls that Sophie had asked to switch her days off so if anything happened, she wouldn't have to leave work.

"All right, girls, eat up so we can get to school!" Sophie was rather happy today. The guy who had turned her life into a living hell ended up behind bars; she was happy and proud of herself for standing up to him, for both her sake and the girls'.

When they pulled up to the school a short while later, the principal was there to greet them. "Good morning, Sophie and Mandy."

"Good morning," they both said together.

"Good morning, girls. I hope you all had a good night's sleep. Are you three ready to learn?"

"Yes, ma'am," the girls said.

"Well, come on, then. Sophie and Mandy, I hope you two have a great day," she said as the kids were piling out of the car.

"Oh, Principal Taylor ..." Sophie ushered her closer to the door so the girls wouldn't hear.

"Yes?"

"I took the day off work in case anything happens, but they should be fine."

"Oh, don't worry. We'll take care of them."

"Thank you. Girls, behave. No more talking to strangers. Have a good day. Love all of you."

"Bye, girls," Mandy said, blowing them a kiss.

The rest of the day went by fine—no phone calls, no worries. Mandy and Sophie decided to do some shopping and run errands. With Sophie's job, it was rare that they ever got to do that. They went to the mall and walked around. They shopped for a few hours and paused to buy a smoothie, sitting down on a bench to relax.

"What time is it?" Sophie asked.

"One twenty."

"Wow. At least we did our shopping. Now do you want to go—"

"Hello, ladies. May I join you?" a male's voice from behind them asked.

"No, thanks," Sophie answered, annoyed and not looking at the man.

"Oh, but, sugarplum, I promise I'll be a good boy."

Sophie turned ghostly white when she realized the man behind the voice. "Harvey, what the hell are you doing here? Why aren't you in prison? Mandy, get your phone ready to call the cops."

"No need to do that. The cops let me go. Since there was no harm done to the children and since I gave my word that I would never hurt them, they let me go. I just have to serve community service, and I'm on probation."

"Whoever the hell was in charge of deciding that should be arrested."

"This has all been fun and everything, but we need to talk about our future together, cupcake," he smirked.

Sophie stood so they were the same height and was about to punch him in the face again when he caught her hand and gave her a little kiss on the nose. "That was so cute," he said.

"How about this?" She kneed him where the sun doesn't shine, and she and Mandy dashed off to the parking lot. They managed to get in the car and drive off. When they were far enough away to feel safe, they slowly relaxed.

"Oh my God, the girls," they both said in horror, and Sophie sped to the school. They wasted no time, both getting out and running to the office.

"Hey, I'm Sophie Smith—Amber, Emily, and Madison Corlow's aunt," Sophie breathed out.

"Yes, ma'am. What can I do for you?" the woman behind the desk asked, clearly a little confused as to what she was running from.

"What rooms are they in?"

"What grades?"

"Amber's in second, and Emily and Madison are pre-K."

"Okay, let me see here. Amber's in room twenty-four, and the other two are in eleven. Would you like a visitor pass?"

"Yes … Actually, can you call them here, please?"

"Checkout?"

"Yes, please."

"All right."

"Also, may I please talk to Principal Taylor? It's an emergency."

"Sure." The woman behind the counter paged the principal and the girls. While Sophie was explaining to Principal Taylor that Harvey somehow only walked away with probation and community service, the girls finally showed up. "We were just about to play a game," Emily said with a pout as she entered the office.

"Yeah, I wanted to play," Madison whined. Sophie, Mandy, and Principal Taylor looked at their crushed little faces and couldn't help but chuckle a little.

"Girls, we're going to go stay at Mandy's for a little bit, like a sleepover," Sophie said, trying to make it sound normal.

"Why? Is that bad man on the loose?" Amber asked.

"Yes, I'm afraid he is, and I don't feel you girls are safe here until he's caught." Sophie and Mandy looked up at Principal Taylor, who just nodded in agreement.

"Okay, girls, come on." They all got up and left, thankful they got there before Harvey. They went back to Sophie's and started rushing to get everything packed. Mandy hurried and helped the twins with their bags; Sophie packed her bag and then helped Amber.

"Phew, we all ready?" Sophie asked, out of breath.

"I think so."

"Perfect. Now let's hurry up and get out of here." They rushed back out to the car, unlocked it, and packed everything in it. "Okay, here we go." Sophie backed the car up, but just when she thought she was almost home free, a car screeched up behind her, making her jerk to a stop. "Oh my God, I'm so sorry. Is everybody all right? That maniac drove up when he saw me pulling out."

She stepped out, ready to give the hooligan a piece of her mind, but then recognized who it was—Timothy, Harvey's younger brother. "Timothy? What the hell were you thinking?"

"Hey, Soph, nice to see you again. My brother gave me sixty bucks to stop you from leaving, and this was the only way I could think of." Timothy grinned as if he'd just achieved a gold medal.

"And it didn't occur to you that you could've killed me, my best friend, and possibly my three nieces in the back seat?"

"You have nieces? I'm sorry. Harvey just said you; he didn't mention kids or anyone else."

"Why would he? Look, I'll give you thirty dollars to move your car out of the way and let us proceed as planned."

"Nope, my brother gave me sixty. Besides, I'm quite comfortable here." He leaned his seat back and propped his feet on the steering wheel.

"Fine. If that's the way you want to play it."

As Sophie turned to go back to the car, she saw the man of her nightmares, Harvey, standing at the driver's side of the car, ready to hop in and take it away. "Harvey ..." Sophie said, trying to calm him down.

"Yes, dear? Hey, Tim. Good job, brother," Harvey said.

"Don't do anything hasty. What do you want?" Sophie asked. Her eyes went to Mandy, who was clearly petrified with fear.

"Oh, honey, I want you. I've always wanted you; you know that. Come." He ushered her over. "Give me a hug."

"Not until you step away from Mandy and the girls."

"Okay, no problem."

He moved about twenty feet into the yard, opening his arms outward, and she slowly walked toward him. When she reached him, he gave her a hug. "Okay, there's your hug. Now will you please tell Tim to move out of my way?"

"Nope. Not quite yet. You see, we still have another six months until we get married, and I can't wait that long for my wonderfully beautiful bride, so I was thinking we get married now."

"Now?" Sophie almost burst into tears, tears of anger, frustration, hate, and horror.

"Yes, now. Or"—he scooted closer to the car—"I'll hit the gas and you can say bye-bye to dear Mandy and the three little brats in the back."

"Mandy knows how to drive."

"Do you think I'm stupid? I've tied up her hands and feet to the passenger door."

"Harvey, you'll pay for this!"

"So do we have a deal?"

"If I say yes, will you let them go, unharmed, and leave

them alone for the rest of their lives, even if you decide to get a divorce."

"Sweetie, I don't ever plan on getting a divorce, but yes, if you agree, no harm will come to the brats or your friend here."

Two minutes went by with complete silence, then three, four, and five minutes more. "Answer me already! I'm getting very impatient, and that gas pedal's looking good right about now." He went toward the car and slowly lowered himself into it, almost hitting the gas.

Sophie shouted, "Fine, you win! I'll marry you. Just please don't hurt them." She fell to the ground and started crying.

"Better." He turned off the car, got out, went over to her, and held her. "Baby girl, why so sad? No need to cry. Look, Mandy and the girls go free and now we can be together just like we wanted in the beginning, remember, pumpkin?"

Sophie shuddered. This man was going to be the death of her …

A couple of hours later, they had packed up all the girls' toys, clothes, and anything else that was theirs into Mandy's car. Mandy's friend Keith had a truck and trailer, and they packed the girls' beds and a couple of dressers as well. Thankfully, Harvey let Sophie help them pack and spend a couple more hours with them before they left. They were saying their last goodbyes. "Is it going to be forever? When can I see you again?" Amber cried.

"I don't know, sweetie, but I promise that you will love living with Mandy. Just keep your head high and be strong for your sisters."

Amber was tired of being told to "be strong"; she was just a child, for heaven's sake. "Okay, I'll try."

Sophie said goodbye to the twins, and Mandy left the driveway. There was no looking back now.

They reached Mandy's pretty neighborhood. There were kids running around and playing outside. There was a small park just down the street and a school a couple of blocks away. "Are we going to go to school?" Amber asked as they passed by the school. This wasn't their school, and Amber feared they might have to switch schools.

"Yes, silly. But you can't go to your old school anymore. This is a new school."

"Why? The bad man won't try to get us anymore, and I promise I'll be good."

"I know that. You girls are good kids. It's just, well, he knows where you girls go to school now, and I don't want anything bad happening again. I would feel like the most terrible person in the world. I know your aunt would want you to be safe, and in order to do that, you must go to school here. Today's Thursday, so you'll start school Monday. I'll have to go up there tomorrow and enroll you three."

"Oh, pretty house!" Emily and Madison both said.

"Yep, this is my house," Mandy said as she pulled into the driveway. "Everybody get out. I don't know where Keith is with the beds, but he should be here soon. Let me go ahead and give you a tour," Mandy added as she and the girls walked in.

"Amber, this will be your room."

"Yay, my own room again!" Amber hugged Mandy.

Mandy couldn't help but laugh. "Yes, you get your own room. It's not as big though. And Emily and Madison ..."

"Yes?" they responded in unison.

"Your room is right over here."

"Yay!" Madison and Emily high-fived each other.

They heard a car horn; it was Keith. "Hey, did anyone order a few beds and a couple of dressers?" he called out.

"Yes, we did." Mandy laughed as they all walked out of the house.

"All right, little lady, where do you want it?" he asked a short time later, referring to Amber's bed.

"Right there." She pointed.

"And your dresser?"

"There."

"Okeydokey."

While he was putting Amber's furniture in her room, the girls had a little snack. "Girls, there are some really nice and friendly kids down the street. When we are done here, we'll go meet them and get you three some new friends. Deal?" Mandy asked. She had a couple of friends who were married and had children around the girls' ages.

"Sounds like fun," Amber said while chewing.

"Okay, I'm done with the little miss's room. Now for the other two. Mandy, want to tell me where to put their beds?"

"Yeah, excuse me, girls."

CHAPTER 11

LIFE WITH MANDY

I t had been a month since the move, and already the girls were having fun. They met some new friends, enjoyed their new school, and had their first sleepover with friends.

Amber asked about her aunt often. Mandy always gave her the same answer: "I'll let you know when I know."

Aunt Sophie hadn't had any contact with them at all in a month's time. *Maybe Harvey took her phone and wouldn't give it back,* Amber thought. Mandy missed her best friend, and Amber missed her aunt terribly. They had to be strong for Madison and Emily though.

"Okay, girls, ready to go play with Katy?" Mandy asked. It was Saturday now, and frankly, Mandy was tired, but she hadn't been able to sleep. The girls had met Katy a couple of weeks ago. Katy's mom and Mandy had been friends for a while now, and she and Mandy would hang out and talk while the girls played.

"Why?" Amber asked.

"Because I have to go to work."

"I thought Aunt Sophie gave you money," Amber said, confused.

"She did, but she stopped."

"Why?"

"Because I don't have to go to her house and watch you anymore. You girls live here now. I've always had a job—it's always when you kids are in school—but I need to work extra hours so we have enough money. So I need you three to go over to Katy's today."

They all climbed into the car and went to Mrs. Love's house. "Hey, Teresa, how are you?" Mandy asked with a big smile when Mrs. Love emerged from the house.

"I'm as good as always. What time do you get off today?"

"Five o'clock. Can you watch them until then? If not, I can probably get someone else to."

"No, they can stay here. Katy needs someone to play with anyway."

"Thank you so much, Teresa. I'll pay you tonight. Bye, girls." She drove off in a rush.

"Okay, girls, come on in. Katy's in her room. Want something to drink?"

"Juice, please," Madison said.

"Go ahead in there. I'll bring it." Mrs. Love was a gorgeous woman with a pleasant personality. She was twenty-five and pregnant. She wasn't that far along yet, but her baby bump was visible. "Here you go, girls," she said, entering Katy's room.

As Katy and the girls continued playing, they heard the doorbell. Mandy couldn't be back already. She'd just left.

They could hear Mrs. Love's excited voice from the living room. "Come here, girls who aren't mine."

Amber, Emily, and Madison left Katy's room.

"Someone's here to see you!" Mrs. Love sounded extremely excited now.

The girls quickened their pace and made it into the living

room. They looked at who was in the doorway. *"Aunt Sophie!"* all the girls shouted. They bombarded her, almost knocking her over. Luckily, she was already kneeling.

"My girls!" she mimicked.

"All right, girls, let's let your aunt come in and sit down," Mrs. Love said. They went to sit on the couch to talk and catch up. That's when Amber asked a question that rather shook Sophie. "Where's Harvey? Is he with you? Please tell me he's not."

"No, Harvey's at home. I told him I was coming over here to visit a few friends. He doesn't know you girls live over here; otherwise, he wouldn't have let me come."

"But you're here. Will you get in trouble?"

"Not if he doesn't find out. I don't plan to tell him. Are you going to tell on me?" Sophie put her bottom lip out and started whimpering. They all laughed.

"No, I pinky promise," Amber said, happy as could be.

"What about you two? Pinky promise you won't tell Harvey?"

"Pinky promise!" they both yelled, and the four of them put their pinkies in the air.

Ding-dong!

"Well now, who could that be?"

"Mandy!" Sophie yelled a moment later.

"Oh my God, Sophie! You're actually here!"

"Of course. I told all of you I would come when I could. I didn't reach out to you because I didn't want Harvey to get mad. He'd probably hit me or something."

"I'd like to see him try to put his hands on you. I'd kill him," Mandy said.

"I love you, Mandy," Sophie chuckled.

"Love you too. Hey, I'm so sorry I can't stay long. I just

brought the girls their stuffed animals from Disney World; they take them everywhere. Here, girls. Sophie, I miss you so freaking much, but I have to go back to work."

"Don't tell anyone I'm here. I don't want Harvey to find out." Mandy agreed and hugged Sophie.

After Mandy left, Sophie asked Mrs. Love if she could pull her car into the garage so no one would see it. Mrs. Love agreed, and they moved their cars. Sophie went back inside to play with the girls and Katy.

Three hours later, Sophie had to go. She hated leaving her nieces, especially now, but she knew they were safe here. She asked Mrs. Love to go out and make sure no one was outside. After that, she went into the garage, got in her car, backed up, and left. She went back home to a very pissed-off Harvey. "Where the hell have you been?" he roared, very upset about something.

"I was hanging with my friends, as I told you."

"I heard you when you said it. What are your friends' names? Do I know them?"

"No, I don't think so. They're Tory, Zoey, and Sam."

"Any guys?"

"No."

"Okay. Well, maybe me, Tory, Zoey, and Sam can meet sometime?"

"Sure, I'll set it up." Sophie had learned a lot in the past month, including how to lie well. She did know a Tory, Zoey, and Sam. They were all people she worked with, and they lived around Mandy.

She went in the bedroom, called them, and arranged the meetup. She and Harvey went to a small restaurant just outside the city and waited for the three to show up. When they did,

Sophie ran over to them and told them to pretend they spent the day together.

"Hello," Harvey said when she introduced them. "I heard you three got to spend the day with my amazing Sophie." Harvey wasn't convinced Sophie really spent the day with these three, and he was determined to get them to admit they didn't.

"Yes, we went shopping and to a movie," Tory said.

"Yeah, we went to the mall and had a great time," Sam added.

"It was good to get out of the office for a while," Zoey said.

"I see." Harvey looked as if he was thinking of something, and Sophie started getting worried.

"So you said you went to see a movie?" he asked Tory.

"Y-yeah."

"What movie did you see?"

Tory looked at Sophie now, seeming panicked.

"Baby, it was just a movie. We went there and pretty much just picked out the first one on the board. We don't remember the name," Sophie said.

She had thought of everything but the fact that she hadn't picked the name of a movie.

"Well then, what was it about?" Harvey crossed his arms.

"It was about two guys."

"And what did they do?"

"They shot someone."

"*Two Guns*," Tory finally said.

"But, sweetie, we just watched *Two Guns* last night."

"R-right."

"Look, we all know you're lying, so why not tell me where you really were?"

"I was with them. We went to the mall, then the movies, and then back to Zoey's house."

"What's Zoey's address?"

"I don't know, but I can show you her house."

"Show me, then. Let's go."

They all got into their respective cars, but Harvey made Sophie drive in front of the other women.

They were just a few blocks from Mandy's house now, and Sophie got scared and turned around.

"Why'd you turn around? I thought it was this street right up here," Harvey said with his usual smirk, knowing something was up.

"It is, but I just want to go home and take a nap. I'm tired."

"Sophie, pull over and let me drive."

She did as she was told, and Harvey got in the driver's seat and turned the car back around.

"What are you doing?" Sophie asked, terrified but trying not to let it show.

"You're hiding something from me, and I want to know what it is. Are you seeing someone else?"

"What? No, never. There's just you."

By now, they were on the street right beside Mandy's house, in between Mandy and Mrs. Love's, where the girls still were. Sophie was sure she was sweating cats and dogs, but she slowly relaxed as they drove down the street. She glanced at Mrs. Love's house and then Mandy's. Mandy was at home, so that meant she had the girls!

"Hmm, well, which is it?"

"What?"

"Your boyfriend's house—which is it?"

"I don't have a boyfriend!" she spat back.

"I think we should go home, then, shall we?" Harvey turned on the next street over, Mandy's street.

Forget cats and dogs; Sophie was drenched in a pool of

sweat now, or so it seemed. It was dark, so she was grateful that the girls wouldn't be outside. Sophie held her breath as they passed her house.

"You know what? I want to go for a walk," Harvey said, and he obviously saw her hold her breath.

Sophie's head started running wild with images. She started to imagine what would happen if the blinds were open and one of the girls walked past and Harvey saw her.

He pulled over to the curb. "Aren't you coming?" Harvey asked, holding her door open. She got out, and he took her hand. "I really like this area," he said after they'd walked for several minutes. "I like how it's not all loud and city-like like your place."

"This *is* a nice area," Sophie said. She thought of her nieces growing up here and how much they must love it.

"Yes, but this house catches my eye the most. Look at the landscaping in the yard and how well it's kept." Harvey was admiring a house just two doors down from Mandy's.

"It's wonderful. Harvey, I'm tired. Can we please go now?"

"Okay, okay, in just a minute."

Still holding hands, they walked closer to Mandy's house. Sophie felt her cheeks getting hot. "Oh, here it is! Is this the house of the person you don't want me to know about?" They were in front of Mandy's house.

"No," Sophie lied.

"All right. Well, I guess you wouldn't mind if I went and knocked on their door?"

"Of course not—go ahead." Sophie stayed on the sidewalk and was silently getting ready to run when someone opened the door.

"Hello, can I help you?" It was a male's voice.

Sophie wondered who it was.

"Hello. My name's Harvey Vince, and this"—he ushered Sophie over—"is my beautiful wife, Sophie."

"Nice to meet you two. Do you live around here? I've never seen you before."

"No, we're from Atchison. We were just with a few friends and decided to do some walking around. This is a nice area."

"Yes, it is. Very beautiful in the spring and summer months, but being October, it's a little nippy tonight."

"Hey, can I ask you a random question?"

"Sure, go right ahead, sir."

"My wife was in this neighborhood earlier with a few friends, and I just want to know if they stopped by here by any chance."

"No, sir. My wife and I live here. We've been here for about three years now."

"May I speak with your wife?"

"Sure, hold on a minute." He went and got his "wife" just as Sophie started looking around and noticed a small window with three little shadows. Then they disappeared.

"Hi, sir, may I help you?" the woman asked.

"I was just asking your husband here if my wonderful wife came by this afternoon."

"No, I'm sorry."

"Well, thank you two for your time. Have a nice evening." He smiled, turned, and took Sophie's hand. They drove home.

"Thank God! Thank you, girls, for being quiet." She then gestured at her friends. "And you two are lifesavers."

Mandy and the girls were happy they hadn't been caught. Luckily, one of her couple friends had come over that night, and when Mandy looked out the window and saw Harvey and Sophie, she had them pretend to live there. "All of you are so welcome," her female friend said. "If you ever need help again, just let us know. We're just down the road. We really have to be going though."

"Okay, thank you two so much. It means a lot."

Mandy waited a few minutes and then let the girls come out of hiding. "Girls, bath and bedtime," Mandy said, exhausted.

CHAPTER 12

HALLOWEEN

I t was Halloween, and the kids were excited. The girls decided to be characters from *The Cat in the Hat*. Mandy had bought Amber a Cat in the Hat outfit, and Emily and Madison wanted to be Things One and Two, so she bought them the outfits and accessories. They spent all day doing fun stuff. They went to the park, the shops, and the movies.

The girls were ready for nighttime so they could go trick-or-treating. This would be the first year they would get to celebrate Halloween. That night, they walked to Katy's so they could all go together. Katy was also excited to go trick-or-treating, but her mom said she was too tired to go out. Therefore, Katy's mom stayed in bed and they started their journey—down one street, up the other side, and on and on.

The girls were having a blast, and Mandy laughed at their little faces when they'd get more candy. The girls noticed a few haunted houses while walking and asked to go through one.

"I don't know; some haunted houses are really scary," she warned them.

"We'll be okay. We'll hold hands," Amber reassured her.

"Fine. If you say so."

They all held hands, Mandy in the middle, Amber on one end, and Katy on the other. It wasn't long before they were inside and screaming, and Emily was getting scared and crying, so they left the haunted house.

"See? I told you haunted houses were scary."

They were done within an hour and decided to call it a night. They took Katy back home and headed back to Mandy's.

"Mandy?" Amber said when they returned.

"Hmm?"

"When do you think we'll see Aunt Sophie again?"

"I don't know, sweetie, but I do know that she loves you very, very much and will do whatever she can to see you three again. I can promise you that you'll see her again. Nobody knows when though." She told the twins to take a bath and get ready for bed. She told Amber that she could watch TV until her sisters were done bathing.

Amber was watching TV in the living room when someone knocked on the door. Amber went and told Mandy, and Mandy looked out the peephole. "Oh, it's just some trick-or-treaters." She laughed and opened the door. "We must've turned the porch light on. Luckily, we have extra candy." She put candy in their buckets before shutting the door and turning off the porch light.

CHAPTER 13
SOMEONE SEES YOU

"**H**ello, Ms. Davis." Principal Ann shook Mandy's hand. "Please come in and sit." Mandy did as she was told, and the principal sat on her side of the desk.

"I asked you to come in today because Principal Taylor called me from Atchison. I know we've spoken about the girls' experience in Atchison; I called you in today to check in and make sure you and the girls are well and there haven't been any incidents."

"No, actually it has been quite uneventful since the last time, with my friends pretending they lived at my house. As I've said before, I can reassure you he won't come up to this school. He has no idea where the girls are located, and he will never find out."

"Ms. Davis, I asked you to come in to let you know that I have spoken with Ms. Smith and Principal Taylor. They said if the girls need anything, here's the number to call." She handed Mandy a piece of paper. "It's Principal Taylor's cell phone number."

"Thank you so much."

"You're so welcome. Also, Ms. Smith wanted you to know

that I have taken Mr. Vince's picture and showed it to each of the girls' teachers, as well as our other staff, and placed the picture in the teachers' lounge."

"This is like a huge weight lifted off my shoulders just knowing the girls are safe."

"I bet it is. It sounds like the girls have had a pretty rough life."

"Oh, you have no idea."

"Okay, well, thank you for your time. We'll make sure the girls are safe; they'll be perfectly fine here." They both stood up and shook hands again.

"I can't thank you enough," Mandy said.

Mandy went back out to her car and then realized how late in the day it was: two thirty. *I might as well wait here then,* she thought. The bell rang, and the girls came outside. Mandy went to get them, and then they headed toward the car.

"Mandy, look!" Amber said, pointing to some trees.

"What?"

"Over there."

Mandy looked but didn't see anything. "What is it?" she asked again.

"Someone's standing over there watching us."

"Girls, in the car—now!" Mandy only saw other kids and their families; she didn't see anyone watching them, but she wasn't about to ignore Amber, especially considering what they'd already been through.

The girls got in the car and hurriedly buckled up. Mandy called the school in fear of walking back in and told Principal Ann what Amber said. They saw Principal Ann walk out and look around. She then walked over to the car and asked Amber where the man was.

"Over there." She pointed again.

Mandy and Principal Ann finally saw him. "He doesn't work here, does he, Principal Ann?" Mandy asked, a little jumpy.

"No, no, he doesn't. Thank you, Amber."

She walked off toward the man, and Mandy began to get a little creeped out. "Excuse me, sir. Hi. I'm the principal of this school. Do you have children who go here?"

"No, ma'am. I have a friend who just picked her kids up. I'd better go say hi."

"Sir, are you talking about that young woman and kids who just got into that car over there?" she asked as she pointed to Mandy's car.

"Yes, ma'am."

"Well, you gave them a fright. Do you know her?"

"Yes, I do."

"Okay, can you stay here a minute, please?"

"Sure thing."

Principal Ann walked back over to Mandy's car. "Mandy, do you know this young man? He says he knows you. Are you two friends?"

"I don't recognize him."

"All right, thank you." She headed back over to the man, and Mandy watched closely.

"Sir, she says she doesn't recognize you. I'm sorry, but I'm going to have to ask you to leave."

"No problem." He turned and went back to his car.

Principal Ann went back over to Mandy's car and told her to wait until he left so he wouldn't follow her home. She sent a police officer out to wait with Mandy in case the man tried anything.

Mandy waited several minutes for the guy to finally leave. When he did, Mandy took off in the opposite direction. When she and the girls got home, she made sure to park her car in her garage so if the man drove by, he wouldn't see it.

"Okay, let me whip something up for dinner," she said.

The girls did their homework, ate about an hour later, played a little, and then went to bed.

Mandy stayed up and looked out her window and peephole a few times. When she felt safe (and exhausted), she went to bed.

The next few days went by smoothly. Their school was more alert now. The principal now stood outside with a police officer before and after school. Mandy dropped the kids off with Principal Ann every morning, and she walked them in. It wasn't the typical way to be escorted into school, but it made Mandy feel much better about the girls' safety.

After a good week, the principal told the cop he could go back to patrolling the traffic, but she remained outside in the mornings and afternoons.

Another week went by, and Mandy relaxed. Principal Ann decided to stay inside the school but keep a watchful eye out. The first day she was in the building, everything went smoothly; second day, same thing; and on and on. Why would that guy come and watch Mandy and the girls leave one afternoon and not come back? They all wondered the same thing.

It was now Christmas break, and they were out of school for two entire weeks. Nothing happened within those two weeks, and Mandy was very thankful. Mandy had her friends over, and most of them brought the girls some toys. They had so much fun, and the weeks went by so fast. Before they knew it, it was the day before school started.

"Okay, wind down," Mandy said as she walked into the

twins' room, where they were all playing. "You have school tomorrow."

"Aww …" Amber and her sisters didn't want Christmas break to end.

"I know, I know. Come on—let's hit the hay."

Principal Ann greeted them the next morning. "Good morning, girls! Mandy … How was Christmas?"

"It was fun!" Amber said with a big smile on her face.

"Did you three get lots of toys?"

"Yes, we did!" All three girls were beaming.

"Good. Will you go inside to your classes, please?" Principal Ann wanted to talk to Mandy alone.

"Any more incidents, Mandy?"

"No, ma'am. Thank God for that."

"Thank goodness. All right, have a good day." Principal Ann waved goodbye as she went back inside.

One week, fine. Two weeks, fine. When three weeks had passed, horror struck.

"Principal Ann, come quick. It's that guy again!"

Principal Ann got up and hurried outside, where the girls were having recess. The three sisters were playing when the guy started walking up to the gate. "Take Amber and her sisters inside to play."

Principal Ann raced to get to the gate. She wanted answers. "Who are you … and why are you watching these girls?"

"Nice to see you again, ma'am. I'm sorry if I came across as being creepy; none of that was intended. Their aunt is my uncle's wife, so in a way, we're all cousins. I don't really know how to introduce myself to them, though, or to their caretaker, Mandy."

"Sir, I don't know if you're telling me the truth or not. But I can tell you for a fact that lurking around is not a good first impression. What's your name? I'll call Mandy and see what she has to say about this."

"I know, ma'am, and I do apologize. My name's Tyler Bell."

"Mr. Bell, I'll call Mandy and tell her what's going on. Do you have a number where I can call you back?"

"Yeah. Do you have paper?"

"I'll put it in my phone. What is it?"

He gave her a number.

"Thank you. I'll call Mandy and call you back. Now, please leave and do not lurk around my school anymore."

"Yes, ma'am."

They both turned to leave each other, and she went straight inside to call Mandy. "Hi, Ms. Davis. How are you today?"

"I'm doing well." Mandy was at work, and Principal Ann could tell she was busy.

"Ms. Davis, do you have a minute?"

"Sure."

"Do you know of a Tyler Bell?"

"Don't think that I do. Is he the mysterious man who was watching us that one day?"

"Yes. So you don't know him? He says the girls' aunt is married to his uncle. Would it happen to be the same aunt they lived with?"

"I don't think so. I don't remember Sophie mentioning anything about Harvey having a nephew. She didn't speak of his family all that much."

"Thank you. I'm going to call Principal Taylor to see if she can get in contact with Ms. Smith and ask her for us. Have a good day."

When they hung up, Principal Ann went to talk with the girls' teachers. "Madison and Emily Corlow are not allowed back out for recess until I say it's all right. When the last bell rings, bring them to my office and I'll escort them out. It's cruel to not let them out, but we have to protect these girls with whatever means necessary." She made the same announcement to Amber's teacher as well.

Principal Ann called Principal Taylor in an attempt to get hold of Sophie, but Sophie was at work, so they had to wait.

Mandy went and picked the girls up from school, being cautious of her surroundings. Principal Ann saw her car pull up and walked the girls out. "All of you have a nice night and I'll see you tomorrow." Principal Ann smiled and closed the door.

"Thank you, Principal Ann," Mandy said before driving away.

Sophie called Principal Ann around seven that night. "Hi, Principal Ann. Sorry, but I can't talk long." Sophie was talking in a low voice.

"Oh, okay. I'll get right to it. Do you know a Tyler Bell?"

"Tyler Bell? No, why? Are the girls safe? And Mandy?" She started to panic.

"Yes, everyone is fine. We had an incident around a month and a half ago where someone was watching Mandy and the girls walk to Mandy's car after school."

"Tyler Bell?"

"Yes, ma'am. We had another incident just today where Mr. Bell was spotted watching the girls at recess. I approached him, and he said he's the girls' aunt's husband's nephew, and I don't know of any other aunt that the girls have."

"No, I'm the only aunt they have. Harvey never mentioned a nephew. I can ask him tonight though."

"Sophie, now I don't want you to get all worked up if Tyler *is* Harvey's nephew. Just remember to stay calm and call me or Mandy immediately."

"Yes, of course. Thank you. I will find out and let you know as soon as I can."

When they hung up, Principal Ann's head was still spinning. What if Tyler was Harvey's nephew and he tried to kidnap the girls? She couldn't allow that to happen, especially not in her school.

The next day, Mandy walked the girls into school so she could talk to Principal Ann. "Good morning, Mandy," Principal Ann said as they approached. "Morning, girls. Why don't you girls go play with your friends inside while we talk? Mrs. Trinity will watch you."

The girls went to play in the halls while Principal Ann and Mandy went into her office. "Is this going to be long, Principal Ann? I don't mean to rush you, but I need to get to work soon."

"This won't take long. I called the girls' aunt Sophie yesterday, and she said she would have to ask Harvey about Tyler. I told her to remain calm and call us immediately, regardless of the answer. But since the girls' only aunt is Sophie, I'm thinking Tyler is Harvey's nephew—that or Tyler's lying and he's no relation to Harvey and therefore is just a creepy young man."

"If Tyler is related, I would have to take the girls out of school and move?"

"Yes, I'm afraid so. We'll do everything we can to help, Mandy. But creepers like him find a way somehow. I've notified the cop who patrols traffic here; he'll keep a watchful eye out. Don't worry too much. We won't know for sure if Harvey's connected until Sophie calls back."

Everything else went smoothly that day. It was four o'clock, and Sophie still had not contacted Mandy or Principal Ann. Mandy started to get nervous and worried. What if Sophie asked Harvey about Tyler and Harvey got mad? Mandy knew Harvey was heartless, but he really cared about Sophie. She hoped he wouldn't harm her physically in any way, but who really knew what a psycho like that would do?

Two hours later, Sophie contacted Principal Ann but got her voice mail. She left her a message. "Hey, Principal Ann. It's Sophie. I asked Harvey about Tyler. Harvey said that Tyler is his nephew but they haven't contacted each other in years. I think he's lying. How else would Tyler know Harvey and I got married—and how would Tyler know about the girls? We just got married five months ago, and the girls only lived with me for about four months. Please notify Mandy as soon as you get this and please keep the girls safe. I'll call back when I can. If something drastic happens, please call Principal Taylor and she will notify me. Thank you."

When Principal Ann got to her phone and heard the voice mail, she immediately called Mandy. "Mandy, hi. How are you?"

"I'm a nervous wreck, honestly. Please tell me Sophie contacted you."

"Yes, she left a voice mail. She said that Tyler is Harvey's nephew, but Harvey said they haven't been in contact for years. She said she didn't believe that because she and Harvey have only been married five months so how would Tyler know about the girls?"

"That's true. In that case, Harvey probably knows where we live, as far as the neighborhood. I've been parking in the garage just in case Tyler does drive around here, and now Harvey probably knows where the kids attend school. When Sophie contacts you again, I want to know why Harvey's spying on the girls. I want to know if they had a fight or something and Harvey wants to hurt them instead of hurting her."

"Okay, Mandy, let me write that down so I'll remember. Got it. All right, I'll be sure to ask Sophie when she contacts me again. Have a nice night, Mandy."

"Thank you."

They hung up, and Mandy got the girls ready for bed.

The next morning was more hectic than before, but it was Saturday, and the girls were out of school and she was home from work, which gave Mandy some time to think. They knew that Tyler was Harvey's nephew, and Harvey was probably aware of the whereabouts of the girls. The only question was, Why? He'd gotten what he wanted five months ago when Sophie had said yes—sort of—and they married. So why was he still after them? Was he after Mandy too? There were so many questions, and the answer was only in the man who caused all this chaos, and the only way to get those needed answers was from Sophie, and frankly, that scared everybody. Would Harvey strike her if she asked? Or would he laugh it off and say they were just crazy accusations she was making up? People didn't usually make up stories about a husband's nephew stalking the wife's nieces. It did sound crazy, but it was happening now and only Harvey knew why.

The girls had fun that weekend. Mandy decided it was best they didn't go far, so they barely went out. They stayed home almost all weekend, except a couple of times, when they went to check on Katy's mom. Mandy did have a few of the girls' friends come over. Before they knew it, it was Sunday night and they were all going to bed.

The next morning, they all woke up, got ready, and went to school. Principal Ann was waiting for them when they got there. Mandy went in with the girls. "Mandy, may I see you for a second, please?" Principal Ann asked.

"Sure."

They went into her office, while the girls waited outside the door. "Look, Mandy, I don't feel the girls are truly safe. Until we hear from Sophie, we don't know why Harvey is having his nephew watch them. I can arrange for two teachers to go to your house with the kids, but that's the best I can do. I really don't like this situation, and I don't want anything to happen to the other students or teachers. It would be my responsibility."

"I understand completely, Principal Ann."

"Good. I think that it's better if the girls stay home and learned, just for a little while. You said Tyler doesn't know where you live, so he won't be able to touch the girls there."

"When will the teachers start?"

"Today, if that's all right with you. I've hired them, and I can call them now and tell them to meet you at your house. They will be there from eight until three or nine until four, whichever you prefer."

"Well, you can call them now and tell them we'll be waiting. Come on, girls."

The girls got up from the chairs and quietly left. "Mandy, why can't we stay in school?"

"Honey, do you remember Harvey?"

"Yes. He's not here though."

"No, he isn't. Amber, this is very complicated. Can you please just do what we say and stay home for a little bit?"

"Okay."

The rest of the ride was silent. Amber wanted to know why she couldn't just go back to school; she wanted to play with her friends and see her teacher. She knew Harvey wasn't there. If he were, Mandy would have made them leave.

They got back to Mandy's and went inside. One of the teachers pulled up right before Mandy shut the door. "Hello. I'm Mrs. Penelope."

"Hi, nice to meet you. I'm Mandy." They shook hands. "Are you Amber's teacher?"

"No, ma'am. I'm not sure who her teacher is; I'm here for the twins."

"Oh, okay, come on in." She moved out of the way and let her in.

"Madison, Emily, come meet your new teacher. You can sit here at the dining room table or go into the living room."

"Thank you, ma'am."

Ten minutes later, Amber's teacher showed up and they started having class. Mandy took off work so she could watch them.

CHAPTER 14
MYSTERY CAR

The next few days went by smoothly, and Mandy started going back to work. On Thursday, as Mandy pulled up to work, something—or rather someone—caught her eye. She couldn't really make the person out because every time she looked in that direction, the person would duck behind some bushes or behind a tree. She called Officer Ryan, the officer at the school, and told him where she was. She locked herself in her car until he got there. She told him there was someone watching her and that he kept ducking when she tried to see who it was.

Officer Ryan told her to go ahead and go to work while he searched the premises. He didn't see anybody. *Maybe Mandy's just loopy from what's been happening this last month,* he thought. He then told her he was leaving and went back to the school.

At four, Mandy got off work and started heading home. She noticed a brownish car following her. She slightly increased her speed, and the car behind her did the same. She couldn't make out whom the driver was. She kept turning in an attempt to lose the car. It didn't work, so she pulled into a friend's driveway and waited. The other car pulled up across the street and parked. She was terrified now. She looked in her rearview mirror; the windows were tinted, and she couldn't see anybody. She called her friend. "Hey, can you do me a weird favor?" she asked.

"Sure, what is it?"

"I'm parked right outside your house. Can you open the front door?"

"Um, sure."

"Thanks." Mandy hung up the phone, and her friend opened the door. She quickly got out of the car and ran inside.

"Mandy, what's up?" James asked, seeming rather stunned to see Mandy like this.

"There's someone following me." Mandy was shaking.

"What? Who's following you?" James asked, going to get her a drink of water to calm her down. She drank it and calmed down a little.

"I don't know. Some person in a brown car."

"Why is someone following you?"

"I don't know. Before I went into work today, I had some creep watching me; I didn't see who it was, though, because the person kept hiding when I looked. I don't know if it's the same person or not. And I didn't want whoever it is to follow me home. Since I was already by your house, I figured I could wait here for a little bit."

"Sure, I don't mind. That person better not stalk me, though, and if he tries coming in, I'll teach him a lesson he won't forget," James said as he flexed his muscles. James was a sweetheart but a total wimp. He and Mandy used to be the best of friends and were super close, but they weren't so close anymore. "Now that I'm okay, I need to call Mrs. Penelope."

"Who's Mrs. Penelope?"

"The twins' teacher." She quickly dialed Mrs. Penelope's number. It rang a few times until she finally picked up. "Hello?"

"Hi, Mrs. Penelope. It's Mandy. Something happened, and I'm going to need you to stay there maybe an extra thirty or forty minutes and watch the girls."

"Is everything all right?"

"Yes, everything's fine. Something just came up. I will pay you for staying later."

"Okay. The girls and I will be waiting."

"Thank you so much. Bye." She hung up and looked at James.

"The girls are at school?"

"No, they're being homeschooled for now. I have to call Officer Ryan now. Hold on."

She dialed Officer Ryan, the cop at the school. "Hey, Officer Ryan, it's Mandy again. I think the same guy creeping on me this morning tried to follow me home. I turned and went to a friend's house instead. The person's driving a light brownish car."

"All right, Mandy. Tell me where you are and I'll come right over."

"Okay. The person's parked across the street on the road, and my car's in the driveway. Can you have another cop come so if he attempts to drive away, he won't get far?"

"Sure. What's the address?" When she told him, he said, "Give me five to ten minutes. I'm on my way."

After ending the call, Mandy dashed over to the door to look out the peephole. She was scared of looking out the window.

"Whoa, what is going on? Is the cop on his way?" James asked. This was all new to him.

"Yes, two cops. He said five to ten minutes."

"See, everything will be fine."

"I don't know if it's the same maniac who spied on the girls and me before ..."

"Wait, what? Someone spied on you and the girls before?"

"Yeah. About two months ago, I went to pick up the girls from school. I went inside and got them, and we were walking back to my car when Amber said she saw someone. I didn't see anybody, but I told the girls to hurry to the car, get in, and buckle up. I called into the school to the principal, who came out. We finally noticed the man. I didn't know him, nor did he work for the school, and the principal told us not to leave until he left. She sent Officer Ryan to sit with us after fifteen minutes. We waited and waited, and he finally left. We waited a few more minutes and then left in the opposite direction."

"Anything else?"

She nodded. "A month after that, the girls were at recess outside and someone started to walk up to the gate. One of the teachers went in and notified Principal Ann. She walked out there, and it was the same guy. She asked what his name was and why he was watching the girls. He didn't give an answer on why he was watching them. He just said his name and that he was the girls' aunt's husband's nephew. The girls only have one aunt, Sophie, and her husband, Harvey. Harvey's the reason the girls now live with me. He threatened to hurt them before if Sophie didn't marry him. And before you say anything, she couldn't go to the police because he said he would for sure hurt them, me, and possibly her too. Anyway, Principal Ann hired teachers, and the girls are now homeschooled until further notice." Mandy let out a breath. That had been a mouthful.

"So let me get this straight: the nephew of the guy who threatened all of you is stalking you four?"

"Yes, and we don't understand why. When Sophie said yes to marrying the crazy psycho, she made him swear up and down he would never lay a finger on the girls or me, even if they were to divorce. They're not divorced. What I need to know is why he changed his mind. Sophie and Harvey have been married five months, so why, after all this time, is he stalking us? I'm starting to wonder if Sophie pissed him off somehow, but I don't blame her for anything that's happened. She didn't know her boyfriend would turn out to be some psychopathic guy who belongs in a mental asylum."

"Sophie said yes?"

"Under her circumstances, yes. Anybody would."

"What were the circumstances?"

"That the girls and I remain unharmed. Okay, well it happened the day the girls moved in with me. Sophie had taken off work—we were both off—and the girls were in school. We went shopping and were going to run errands, but we didn't get that far. We were at the mall and decided to take a break from all the shopping. We sat on a bench with all our bags and just started chitchatting. Well, this guy came and sat behind us. We couldn't see who it was 'cause we were facing forward. The guy started to talk to us, and we kind of just shook it off. Sophie recognized the voice, and we turned around to see Harvey. Harvey was supposed to be in jail because the day before that, he attempted to kidnap the girls at school—just scooped them up in his arms and started to run. The principal ran after him and called the cops. The cops stopped him, and the principal got the kids back to school safe and sound. Sophie went to the police station and said Harvey was looking at prison time. But while at the mall, Harvey told us that the cops supposedly said since the girls weren't hurt in any way, he just had probation and community service. Obviously, Harvey doesn't follow the law, because in the beginning of October, he and Sophie were strolling along this area for reasons I don't know.

"Anyway, Sophie kneed him in his guy parts, and she and I made a run for it. We made it to the car and started driving when we realized the girls were probably about to be in danger. So Sophie sped to the school. We got the girls out, brought them back to the house, and started packing as quickly as we could. We threw our bags in the car and everyone got buckled in. Sophie started the car and had started to back out of the driveway when Harvey's little brother sped up and parked his car right behind hers.

"Sophie got out to talk to him, and the girls and I stayed buckled in the car. I started talking to the girls, hushing them, and next thing I know, I was hit over the head with something. When I came to, Harvey was standing in the door of the driver's side talking to Sophie, and the girls were in the back, scared as can be. I looked down and noticed someone had tied my hands and legs to the door and put something over my mouth. My head still hurt terribly. I couldn't really hear anything that well, but I remember seeing Harvey get in the car, put it in reverse, and slowly pull his foot off the brake. I guess his brother, Tim, had moved his car out of the way.

"I remember Sophie screaming, 'Fine, you win; I'll marry you! Please don't hurt them.' Then Harvey put the car back in park and went over to her. Sophie came over, her face all red, looked at me, and started untying me. She said, 'I'm so sorry, Mandy,' and then she went and unbuckled the girls. We all went inside, and Harvey said she could say goodbye to us and help the girls pack. So that's what we did. I called Keith over, and he got the girls' beds and dressers on his truck and trailer. When we were all done, we said our goodbyes and the girls and I left."

The doorbell rang. Mandy rushed to the door and answered it.

"Hello again, Mandy." It was Officer Ryan.

"Hey, Officer Ryan. Come on in."

"Thank you. So … the person in the light brown car says he knows you."

"I don't know anyone who drives a light brown car. Was it Tyler?"

"No, ma'am. I would definitely recognize him. This gentleman was younger, maybe eighteen."

"I'm afraid I don't know of any eighteen-year-old."

"Mandy, how old is Timothy?" James cut in.

"I'm not sure. Harvey's twenty-nine, so he's not much younger than that. Do you think it might've been him?"

"I don't know. Did you see his car that day?"

"Yes, I got a glimpse of a little gray car, not light brown."

"Maybe Harvey's switching up cars and playing mind tricks with you."

"Not sure. Maybe."

Officer Ryan jumped back in the conversation. "Mandy, we talked to the young man, and he said something about pulling a prank on you. He had a dash cam that was recording. Very odd."

"I don't think he was trying to prank me, Officer Ryan. I don't know—I guess we're stuck. We don't really have anything. I guess you can leave now."

"Yes, ma'am. Are you going to leave as well? If so, I could follow in my police car."

"Yes, just give me a minute."

"No problem." Officer Ryan stepped outside, and Mandy turned to James. "Thanks, James." Mandy hugged him.

"No problem. If you need anything, I'm just a phone call away."

She left, and Office Ryan escorted her back to her house with no problems. She told Mrs. Penelope she could go, and then she made dinner for the girls. "Did you have fun learning today?" she asked them.

"Yeah, I did!" Emily exclaimed.

"Me too!" Madison grinned.

"It was fun," Amber said.

"Good, I'm glad you enjoyed it. Now eat up so we can shower and go to bed. Tomorrow's Friday!"

"Yay!" all three girls shouted.

Mandy didn't want to get out of bed the next morning She'd had a nightmare that the man had followed her into her house and taken the girls. She'd woken up and checked on them. She knew it was a just a dream, but after what had been happening, who wouldn't be jumpy?

Mrs. Penelope rang the doorbell, and Mandy groaned. She finally got up and let both the teachers in. "Hey, Mrs. Penelope." Mandy yawned. "Hey, Ms. Scott, come on in."

"Thank you, Mandy. Are you all right?" Mrs. Penelope asked.

"Yeah. Restless night—that's all."

"Okay, dear. Are the girls up yet?"

"They should be. Let me go get them." She went and got the twins first, then Amber. She cooked breakfast for all of them, and they went straight to the whiteboards that the school had generously donated. Soon after she ate, Mandy had to get ready for work. She just thanked God it wasn't her day to open. She got dressed and ready for the day tiredly, kissed the girls, and left.

So far, so good. No one was spying on her today. Four hours into work and it was lunchtime. She got an hour for lunch, and she went to spend it with the girls. She went back to work, and everything was still fine. She relaxed and focused on work the rest of the day.

"Six o'clock finally!" Mandy said to no one in particular.

She went out to her car, hoping no one would follow her home that day. She laughed and shrugged it off. At least she was off tomorrow. She started her car and left. She glanced in her rearview mirror and didn't see anything, so she continued on her path home. She was on her street when she saw the same mysterious light brown car parked a few houses down from hers. *What are they doing here?* she wondered.

The person in the car watched her as she continued driving up the street in an attempt to find out where she lived. She'd seen the car, so she drove past her house and called Mrs. Penelope. "Hi, Mrs. Penelope, don't be alarmed, but there's a car a few houses down that was, uh, stalking me yesterday, which was why I was late. I'm going past my house now. Can you have the girls stay away from the windows? I'm going to drive around a little and try to lose this car."

"Would you like me to call the cops?"

"No. I will if I need too. Can you park in the street so I can pull into my garage?"

"Will do. Please be careful, sweetie."

Mandy went down one street, then another, until the driver of the light brown car gave up and drove away. Mandy went back to her house after her little follow-the-leader game. She pulled into the garage, went inside, and paid Mrs. Penelope for babysitting during after-school hours. "Bye, Mrs. Penelope. Have a good night."

She approached the girls. "Hey, girls, hungry?"

"Yeah!" they all said.

"Go watch TV or something; I'll make dinner."

Later, after the kids went to bed, Mandy thought, *TGIF*.

Mandy's phone started ringing around eleven the next day. She didn't recognize the number, so she ignored it. It rang again, the same number, and she still ignored it. It rang a third time, and she answered.

"Hey, Mandy!"

"Hey, Sophie! I didn't recognize the number."

"Oh, sorry. I forgot your rule about not answering unknown numbers. This is a coworker's phone."

"Yeah. Especially with what's been happening lately."

"What's been happening?"

"A lot. What's up?"

"I talked to Harvey, sort of, and he asked how I knew about Tyler. I told him that I found out about Tyler through the police. See, the police asked if I knew of any relatives of Harvey's because for some reason, they lost all his information *mysteriously.*" Sophie and Mandy both rolled their eyes. "I told them I only knew his brother, that I didn't know of any other relatives; he didn't talk about them. I told them they would probably just have to run his name. They did and found out about his sister and Tyler."

"Who's his sister?"

"Laura Vince Bell-Miller."

"Never heard of her."

"Well, the address on file is a town five hours from you."

"Then ... Tyler doesn't live here?" Mandy asked.

"Nope. Five hours away. I tried to come up with the words to ask Harvey why his nephew was spying on you, but that would make it sound like a psycho who knew where you lived, so instead, I just asked him if he would ever harm the girls or you. He asked why I would bring that up because he swore he never would once we were married. I said I knew, that it was just a thought I had."

"So he didn't admit to spying on us?"

"Why would he?"

"I don't know. But we do know that Tyler doesn't live here, according to the file."

"He might; he might've moved out of his mother's house," Sophie replied.

"True. I have a cop here who knows the girls and me and knows our story. Do you think it would be safe to talk to him? Maybe get him to find out something more?" *And while he's doing that, he could find out who's been following me*, she thought.

"Okay, sure. You could talk to him."

"Hey, Sophie, I have a question."

"All right, but I only have a little bit longer."

"Has Harvey's brother visited you lately?"

"He's been staying with us, but he left a few days ago."

"How old is he?"

"Eighteen. Why?"

"No reason. Got to go."

Sophie was confused. Why the sudden interest in Harvey's brother? Was that where he went? Was he checking in on Sophie and the girls too? She had to figure this out, and she knew she was the only person who could.

CHAPTER 15

SOMEONE WICKED THIS WAY COMES

fter those few scares, Mandy was worried that she'd have to either move or let the girls go, for their own good. She really didn't want to do either. She and the girls had many friends here, not to mention the principal, who thankfully communicated through Sophie and Mandy when necessary. She wasn't sure she wanted to share the girls' story; people would look at her as if she'd just gotten off the bus to crazy town, not that she cared. Now she knew that Timothy and Tyler were in her town for some reason, and she wasn't positive, but they were probably watching her and the girls for Harvey. It scared her. At least the girls were at home all the time now; it made it much easier to keep an eye on them.

Two weeks went by, and there were no more incidents. Mandy still didn't let her guard down. She remembered that the last time they did that, Tyler spied on the girls while they played at recess. She wasn't worried about Tyler much anymore. She guessed Harvey knew she knew about Tyler and so sent

Timothy in a mystery car to spy. She hadn't seen that car for weeks, not that she missed it—no creepy car or Tyler. Every day when she came home, she parked in the garage so no one would see the car, and they didn't leave the house much now.

"Mandy, please, I want to go to the park," Amber begged.

"Amber, you know I would love to take you girls, but we can't." It had now been a month of no incidents, but Mandy still wasn't fully trusting of her town. She hated disappointing the girls, but she knew it was for their own safety.

"But why?"

"Amber, honey, you're still too young to understand, but we have to stay here. Go get your jacket and play in the backyard. I'll go with you." Mandy took the three girls out to the back so they could play. She had bought a play-yard and bicycles for the kids, and as long as an adult was present, they could go out and play whenever they wanted. She had also installed a tall wood fence so no one could look in and spy.

Ring!

Mandy answered the phone.

"Mandy, hi; it's Harvey. Don't hang up."

Mandy was terrified but also curious as to why Harvey was calling. Did he know that Sophie had come to see them and was he mad about it?

"Mandy, are you there?"

"Y-yeah. What do you want?"

"I'm sorry to tell you this, but Sophie's really sick and is in the hospital. She wants you and the girls to come see her. She fears the worst. She can't talk, so she had me call. She's also asleep right now, so I had the opportunity to leave the room and do so."

"How do I know you're not lying?"

"Mandy, why would I lie about something like this? Sophie wrote me asking me to call and get you all down here. She also told me about going to visit you four, but I don't care about that right now. You know me though. If you four aren't here in an hour, I will personally send a car for the girls. And I don't think you want me to do that. I have to go talk to the doctors. Bye now."

Mandy was scared and confused but tried not to let the girls see it. *Sophie would FaceTime with us even if she couldn't talk,* Mandy thought. *Nothing would stop her from seeing the girls. Maybe I'll call the hospital to see if his story's right.*

She called the main hospital and three others around Sophie's city, but they all told her there wasn't a Sophie or Harvey there.

Hmm, Mandy thought. *I know Harvey cares for Sophie, and I don't think he would lie about her being sick. But they're not in any hospital around here, and he does know that Sophie came to visit. Did he do something to her? I swear to God—*

Amber interrupted her thoughts. "Mandy?"

"Yeah?"

"You look mad. Are you okay?"

"I'm fine, honey. Go play some more."

"All right ..." Amber was smart and knew something was wrong, but she went to play anyway.

"*Psst.*"

Mandy looked around but didn't see anyone.

"*Psst.*"

The sound came from behind her now. She looked around again but still saw no sign of anyone.

"Girls, come on. Let's go back inside."

"Aw." The girls all sighed but followed Mandy's orders.

"*Psst.*" The sound was coming from inside the house now. Mandy looked over at the house but didn't see anyone.

"Girls, if that's one of your dolls, I swear I'm going to throw it away," Mandy said, laughing at herself.

"If what's one of our dolls?" Amber asked.

"That *psst*-ing sound. Do you hear it?"

"No."

Mandy thought that maybe it was just her imagination, that everything was fine.

Bam! The noise came from the kitchen. Mandy and the girls jumped.

Mandy told Amber to stay in the room with her sisters while she went to investigate. Mandy grabbed a candlestick and her phone, with Officer Ryan's number pulled up, and crept into the kitchen.

"What the hell are you doing here?" Mandy asked James. "And why did you scare me like that? I almost called the cops!" Mandy lowered her phone and the candlestick.

Amber and her sisters entered the kitchen and greeted James.

"Hey, girls. Oh, and I'm sorry. I didn't mean to scare you ladies. I just needed to borrow a pan."

"And why didn't you call? And more importantly, how the hell did you get in my house?"

"I did call. Your new boyfriend said he would deliver the message, and I have a key, remember?" He waved his keys up.

"Oh, right." Mandy felt so foolish. She had forgotten she'd given James a key when she changed her locks. "What boyfriend?" She didn't have a boyfriend, nor was anyone else in the house.

"He answered your phone earlier, said his name was Lewis. Said you two had just gotten together not too long ago but he was staying over here to watch after you and the girls ... You do have a boyfriend named Lewis?"

"James, I don't know a Lewis, and if I did, I would tell you about him." Mandy was starting to freak out. She looked at her cell phone for an answer. She scrolled through her texts and recent calls. "There's a call from you from early this morning, but I was still asleep. I'm really freaked out now."

Suddenly, she heard the sound of clapping hands from the hall.

"Good show! You know, you really are a great friend and semismart," a male's voice said as he walked into the kitchen. He was about twenty-four, tall and muscular but thin. He had blond hair, green eyes, and was dressed in a T-shirt and pants.

Mandy didn't recognize him. James and Mandy grabbed the girls and put them behind them.

"Who are you?" Mandy asked. "And why and how are you in my house?" James and the girls looked terrified now.

"My apologies, darling. I'm Lewis," he said with a mischievous smile.

"What are you doing here?" Mandy asked again. She didn't like it when random people showed up at her door, let alone in her kitchen.

"Just in the neighborhood and thought I'd say hi."

"Okay, smart-ass. Who the hell are you and why are you in my house? I want the truth."

"Whoa, babe, calm down. I'm Lewis, your boyfriend. I live here with you and your friend's nieces. You don't remember 'cause I wiped your memory." Lewis laughed. "The truth is that I'm here to kidnap the girls and take them to Harvey and Sophie, so if you will gladly hand them over ..." He stepped closer. Mandy and James put the girls farther behind them and stepped back themselves.

"Where did you come from? Why would you want to kidnap them? And again, how did you get in my house!"

"Well, I was born over in Australia and moved to the States when I was seven—"

"Look, you piece of shit, just answer the questions!" James was furious.

"Whoa, calm down. What got in your coffee this morning? I live about three hours from here. My cousin called earlier and said he needed a favor, so I came to the rescue. Oh, and I picked your lock. Nice place you have, by the way—very homey."

"I'm guessing the favor was to kidnap the girls," Mandy said, more like she knew than if she were asking a question. "Yes, ma'am. And my cousin isn't very patient, so if you would just hand them over, I'll be on my way and you'll never see me again." He leaned up against the wall.

Mandy and James grabbed the girls' hands. "You're going to have to kill us to get to them," James said.

"I don't want to kill anyone. How brutal is that? Jeez. That's definitely not how I roll."

"I'm sorry, but you have to leave. You're not getting these girls—or anything else, for that matter—so please leave." James was trying to be calm and civil.

"Okay, fine. But like I said, my cousin's not patient; I don't think you'll like what he has planned."

"And what exactly does he have planned?"

"Oh, well, I'm sure you already know who my cousin is. You know Harvey, right, Mandy? He said you two have a history and he hates your guts now, so I have come to get the girls and gladly transport them over to him and their lovely aunt, but if you don't cooperate, Harvey's planning on getting you for kidnapping—and possibly murder—and sending you away for a long time."

"He can't do that! I have legal custody of these girls. Sophie even signed the papers. He was there!"

"That's true. But he said that the papers were mysteriously destroyed, and now there's no evidence that you have rights to these girls."

"Goddamn it, Harvey," Mandy whispered under her breath.

"Yes, so I'll take the girls now." Lewis motioned for the girls.

"What are Harvey's plans?"

"I really don't know. I'm just the messenger boy. Which reminds me, Harvey said to give the girls up or he'll blow your house up. Now, I doubt you'll want to see that happen. Then we all die, and I'm only twenty-five. I have my whole life ahead of me, as do the five of you. So it's your choice. You have about eight hours to decide and say goodbye to the girls. Sleep on it; I'll be watching TV." Lewis went into the living room and turned on the TV.

"How do we know for sure that you're telling the truth?" Mandy asked, walking closer to Lewis.

"Why doesn't anyone ever believe me? Look." He pulled out his phone to display a picture. "Here's the bomb. It has a timer that will go off in about eight and a half hours. It can't be disarmed so don't even try; if you do, we'll all blow up."

Frightened, Mandy went back in the kitchen.

"James, I'm so sorry you got dragged into this, but can you please help? I don't know what to do anymore."

"Mandy, you're my best friend. I'm not going anywhere." James smiled and hugged her.

"Okay, so what do we do? We can either stay here and get killed with the girls or do as he says and release them."

"Mandy, I love you and these girls; I couldn't imagine my life without you four. If we stay here and refuse to hand them over, then yes, we will all die. There's always a possibility that no harm will come to the girls if we let them go. You heard him; he doesn't kill."

"Yeah, but what about Harvey? The way his mind works, he'd kill them in front of Sophie just to watch her pain."

"I doubt it. Harvey promised you and Soph that he wouldn't touch a hair on the girls' heads, right? Maybe he just wants to reunite a family."

"You're right, and then right after that, he'll take them out for ice cream." Mandy was getting tired of James being so naive. "For unknown reasons, Harvey hates those girls, and the second he gets them in his grasp, he'll ship them off, literally."

"You're right. Mandy, I know you love those girls and would die for them, but if you die, they die."

"And if I live, they die. So either way, we all lose."

"Not necessarily." James smiled a little.

"Do you have something planned?"

"Let's all go to Amber's room and pack," he whispered to all of them.

"All right, here's the plan," James said as they sat in the room.

"Hold on," Mandy said, turning on the radio to drown out their voices.

"I plan on letting the girls go ..."

"But—"

"Let me finish. I plan to let them go back with Lewis. They'll all be in the car, and the girls will claim they have to go the bathroom. They'll stop, and all three girls will go in at the same time. We'll show up in the back and grab them. We'll be in and out before Lewis knows what happened."

"That plan sounds a little iffy to me—and how do we know Lewis will even stop?"

"I don't know. Just guessing. It's the best thing I can think of, and it's the only plan we've got."

"I don't know. Amber's only seven, and the twins are four. Amber's intelligent, but do you think she and her sisters could do this alone? Maybe we should just call the cops."

"Mandy, if we do that, Harvey could set off the bomb early. This is the only way that we can all make it out alive and the only way the kids will be safe with us."

"Okay. I'm trusting you."

They started packing, and Mandy went into the living room. "Will Harvey blow up my house?" Mandy asked Lewis, who was still watching TV.

"Harvey didn't give me any details, just told me to get the girls. I'm not entirely sure about your house. I just know you have around eight hours before that thing goes off, and I don't want to be here when it does. I don't think you and lover boy over there want to be here either."

"All right."

Mandy went upstairs and started packing a suitcase for herself. "James, I might have to stay with you for a while."

"That's fine. Stay as long as you want." He smiled at her.

They finished packing and took a nap. Two hours left …

"Here, Amber." Mandy handed her a flip phone. "When you, Emily, and Maddie get into the gas station bathroom, I want you to hit this button twice. It will call James and me, and we will come get you, all right?"

"Okay, Mandy." Amber was nervous and kind of excited at the same time. She had to be a big sister and bodyguard for her sisters.

They put all their stuff in the cars. One hour left …

Mandy was telling the girls goodbye, with Lewis watching

carefully. "Well, I guess this is goodbye, Amber. I love you so much. Be brave. You three be good for Mr. Lewis." Mandy was now hugging them. "Listen to him and mind your manners like the good girls you are, okay? I don't know when I'll see you again. I love you." Mandy started sobbing as she held Amber and her sisters.

"Don't worry, Mandy. I'll take good care of them. I'll even have Harvey call you after I drop them off so you know we got there safely." Lewis grinned. Mandy rolled her eyes.

"Bye, Mandy. I love you," Amber said, crying. The twins started crying too.

Mandy hugged them all one more time. "This won't be for long, I promise. Just remember the plan," she whispered in Amber's ear.

"All right, let's go, girls," Lewis guided them to the car and buckled them in.

Mandy and James stood there watching as a maniac took her three sweet girls away.

CHAPTER 16

THE PLAN

"The itsy bitsy spider went up the water spout ..." Lewis, Amber, Madison, and Emily were all singing loudly to the music. The girls were actually having fun, but not so much that Amber forgot the plan. "Down came the rain and washed the spider out," they all continued. Amber hadn't yet seen the gas station Mandy told her about, and she was worried they'd passed it.

"So, girls, are you happy to see your aunt again?" Lewis asked, turning the music down.

"Yes!" Madison and Emily shouted. Amber was thinking about the plan. "Amber, are you all right?" Lewis asked.

"Yeah. I just have to go to the bathroom. Can we stop?" Amber had seen the sign and felt relieved.

Lewis pulled into the gas station lot, and Amber took Madison and Emily with her to the bathroom. She took the flip phone out of her pocket and followed Mandy's directions. "Hey, James, we're here."

"Perfect, sweetie. We'll be there in a few minutes; we were carefully following his car."

"Okay."

Five minutes later, they heard a banging on the door. "Someone's in here!" Amber said.

"It's us, baby. Hurry and open the door." Mandy was there. The girls opened the door and exited the restroom.

"Let's get out of here," James said, gripping Madison's and Emily's hands. They ran out to his car and piled in.

They didn't get too far before Lewis realized what happened and tracked them down. "That was a mistake, Mandy," Lewis said under his breath. He followed closely behind, pulling out his phone and dialing a number. "Harvey, I had them, but Mandy and her friend decided to double-cross me. They made a plan with the girls, and they came and got them from this gas station. They snuck out of the bathroom. I know. I'll get them back. All right, I got it. Thanks, Harv."

He sped up until he was next to them. "Okay, Mandy and James, let's see how well you like this." Lewis tried to swerve them off the road but was careful because of the girls.

"Damn it," James cursed. "Mandy, he's not easing up." James then sped up in an attempt to lose him.

James's phone started going off. "What!" he answered. He could hear laughing on the other end.

"Oh, pretty boy, do you really think you can beat me? 'Cause you can't. Oh, and tell Mandy her house, car, and work are gone. Harvey's words, not mine."

"What do you mean 'gone'?" James spat.

"I mean gone, burned up. Luckily, there wasn't anyone at her work … that I know of anyway." James hung up.

"Who was that?" Mandy asked, still scared.

"Lewis. He said Harvey told him that your house, car, and work burned up."

"Let's beat this asshole."

James and Lewis swerved back and forth, trying to run

each other off the road. Lewis hit James just right, and his car flipped—once, twice, and then three times. Lewis actually felt bad. Not only for Mandy and the girls but also for himself. He couldn't live with the guilt if he'd killed someone. He raced off the road and ran down to the car. "Hello? Girls!"

After what seemed like forever, he heard a little groan. "Amber?" He reached in, opened the door, carefully removed her, and laid her on the ground. He then looked back at the other girls, who looked asleep—or at least that's what Lewis hoped was the case. He loaded the girls in his car and was getting ready to drive off when *bam*! James's car went up in flames, and parts went flying everywhere. Lewis felt bad but hopped in his car and drove off.

Ten minutes later, he calmed down a little and called Harvey. "Hi, Harvey. I got the girls, but we had a little accident. Can you meet us at the hospital?"

"What the hell happened?" Harvey was clearly upset.

"I tried to chase them off the road like you said. But I guess I got too worked up about it and accidentally made James's car flip, and now the girls are … well, I'm not really sure. Amber woke up and groaned a little but then passed out again."

"So what happened to Mandy and James?"

"The car exploded after I got the girls out. They're … gone."

"Okay … I guess I'll deal with that later. I'll see you soon."

An hour later, Harvey arrived at the hospital where Lewis had taken them. "Lewis, tell me the girls are fine."

"They're fine. They just woke up. Come on—I'll take you to them."

"Hi, girls. Remember me?" Harvey asked, smiling.

"What are you doing here? Where's Aunt Sophie?" Amber asked, trying to push the little red button she knew was for the nurse.

"Something happened, but don't worry—you girls will be fine."

Harvey then walked out in the hall to talk to Lewis. "Thank you for your help, Lewis. Here's the money I promised ... and a little extra for your car's damage. The girls don't know the truth about Sophie, do they?"

"No. I didn't tell them anything."

"All right, good. You can go now."

"Excuse me—when can the Corlow girls go home?" Harvey asked a nurse at the station.

"What's your name and relationship to them, sir?" she asked, typing away at her computer.

"Harvey Vince. They're my nieces by marriage. I heard about the horrible wreck that they were involved in and came by to see them. Their aunt misses them terribly and wants to see them soon; she's really sick and can't make it here, so I told her I would take them."

"Will you just fill out this paperwork? The man who dropped them off just gave me the girls' and your name, stating that you are indeed their uncle, and they may be released tomorrow afternoon. We're keeping them overnight for observation."

"Okay. Thank you." He grabbed the paperwork and went to sit down.

"We interrupt this TV broadcast for a news announcement." Harvey immediately turned his attention to the TV. "Authorities are saying a car flipped over several times and burned. Two people were found burned in the front seat. They aren't sure if the deaths were prefire or not. There were also three booster seats in the back seat, but no kids. The back door was reportedly open, but cops say that could be from the explosion. Authorities say helicopters and squad cars were sent out, but there aren't any signs of the kids. They are stating that right now this may be a hit-and-run, murder, and possible kidnapping. Police say that the car had suitcases in it, possibly for a family getaway or move. The two adults in the front seats have yet to be identified. No other news at this time."

"Damn it, Lewis," Harvey whispered under his breath.

"Hi, Amber, Madison, and Emily. Are you girls ready to see your aunt Soph?" Harvey asked the girls the next day. The girls were now out of the hospital, and they were all in the car heading to Sophie's.

"Yes." Amber was scared of Harvey. "How much longer?"

"Just half an hour—thirty minutes."

Forty-five minutes later, they arrived at Sophie's house. "Yay!" the girls screamed.

"Where's Sophie?" Amber asked.

"She's inside, of course. She's very ill." Harvey got the girls out of the car, and they all ran to the door. After Harvey unlocked it, the girls rushed inside. "Sophie!" Amber called her name as she ran through the house. "Soph?" Amber hurried back over to Harvey. "Where is she?"

"She's in that room." He pointed to the master bedroom.

Amber took her sisters' hands, and they slowly went inside. "Sophie?" she said as they entered the room. "Hey, she's not in here. Where is she?" Amber was getting scared.

"She's right there." Harvey pointed to the bed.

"No, she's not ..." Amber was terribly confused.

"You see, your aunt got very sick, and sadly, she passed away." Harvey looked sincerely sad.

"*No!* She didn't. What did you do to her!" Amber burst into tears and started hitting him.

"Amber, I didn't do anything to her. She was my whole world."

"Why did you bring us here?" Amber asked.

"Sophie wanted to see you one last time."

"But she's not here."

"Yes, she is."

The crazy psychopath thought she was lying on their bed. Amber looked around the room; it looked the same as it had when they'd lived there, only it felt sad and cold. "Harvey, I don't see her. She isn't here. Where's Mandy and James?"

"Listen to me. I didn't mean to kill Mandy and James."

"Y-you what! They died?" Amber started hysterically crying now.

"Amber, I didn't mean for that to happen. I know it's hard to think about and you're too young to know, but your aunt Sophie meant everything to me. It's true I didn't like Mandy, and I didn't know the guy she was with in the car, but that didn't mean I wanted them to die. If they would've just let you come here with Lewis, everything would've been fine."

Harvey had changed somehow; Amber could see it in his face. "Harvey, what's going to happen to us?"

"I'm going to have to take you to the police because you can't stay here."

"What are they going to do?"

"I don't know." Harvey led the girls outside to his car.

They rode to the police station in silence. When they went inside, a police officer asked, "May I help you?"

Officer Grant emerged from a back room. "Amber?"

"Officer Grant!" Amber and the girls ran to hug him, and he kneeled down. "What's going on?" he asked as he looked up to see Harvey. "Who are you?"

"Hello, sir. My name is Harvey Vince. I was the girls' aunt Sophie's husband. You have heard of her passing?"

Officer Grant led them over to his cubicle and started

looking for their file. "I have, and she contacted us when the girls went to live with Ms. Mandy Davis."

"Yes, um, I have sad news; can you have the girls go somewhere else, please?"

"Sure." He got a female officer to take them back to play.

"These girls are special, and their aunt was the best thing that's happened to me, but I've done some really bad things and am ready to turn myself in and suffer the consequences."

"Okay, Mr. Vince. What exactly did you do—and why are these girls involved?"

"It started when they moved in with Sophie." He went on to tell about the proposal and her giving up the girls to Mandy because he didn't like kids. "Let me get this straight: you threatened to hurt the girls if their aunt Sophie wouldn't marry you?"

"Yes, sir. But there's a lot more."

"Just sit tight. I'm going to get the sheriff."

Officer Grant headed into Sheriff Ziree's office and explained to him what Harvey had just told him.

"Will you show him to my office?" Sheriff Ziree was interested to hear what else Harvey had done.

Sheriff Ziree stood and shook his hand when he entered. "Hello, Mr. Vince. Officer Grant, where are the girls?"

"They're out here with Officer Leah."

"Very good. Thank you."

Officer Grant then left the two alone, and they sat.

"So, Mr. Vince, Officer Grant tells me that you admitted to threatening to harm the girls if their aunt didn't marry you. Is that correct?"

"Yes, sir. I know it was wrong, and now that I look back at it, I never should've threatened anybody. I wasn't in the right state of mind at that point in my life. I was taking medications, which is no excuse. I knew that if I had threatened them, Sophie would have to get rid of them and she'd be mine forever."

"Okay. Tell me about the other stuff you did. Why do you have the girls? Officer Grant gave me the girls' file, and it says here that they were left to a Ms. Mandy Davis, signed by the girls' aunt Sophie Smith."

"Yes, sir. To know why I have the girls, you need to know everything else first. This may take a while."

"No problem. Can I get you some water or coffee?"

"No, thanks."

"Okay then, you may proceed."

"Thank you, sir. If you look in my file, you'll see that I have been in here before. I attempted to kidnap the girls before, at their school. Officer Mason took the case, but the station let me go because the girls weren't ever in harm."

"I see." The sheriff located his file.

"After the station let me go, I went to see my fiancée, Sophie. I found her and Ms. Davis at the mall. Sophie knew that I was the one who attempted to kidnap the girls, so as you can imagine, she was furious with me." Harvey was starting to tear up at the thought of his beautiful deceased wife.

"Here you go." Sheriff Ziree gave Harvey a Kleenex. "So what happened after you saw them?"

"I told Sophie that they gave me probation, but Sophie and Mandy didn't want anything to do with me. I didn't care much for Mandy to begin with."

"Is it because Sophie spent so much time with her?"

"Yes."

"So then what?"

"I knew that after that, Sophie would want to get out of this city as soon as possible, and I just couldn't let that happen. I called my brother and asked if he would stop them from leaving. I never thought that he would almost run them over. She was pulling out of the driveway, and he blocked her. I also didn't think of Mandy or the girls being in the car. I knew that if I wanted to keep Sophie, I needed to think fast. I honestly don't know why I did what I did next. The girls have a T-ball set, and I saw a bat on the ground, so I picked it up and hit Mandy with it. I didn't expect her to pass out, but she did. I tied her hands and feet to the passenger door. I then proceeded to walk over to the driver's side and stand just inside the door as I was talking to Sophie. I knew she'd never even think of staying, so I again threatened to harm the four people she loved most in this world.

"I lowered myself into the car and pulled it out of park; by then, my brother was gone. I eased my foot off the brake just enough for the car to move an inch, and Sophie agreed to marry and stay with me as long as no harm came to Mandy or her nieces. So I turned the car off, ran over to Sophie, and gave her a hug. I then let her untie Mandy and get the girls out of the car."

"Mr. Vince, correct me if I'm wrong, but there were two incidents where you threatened Mandy and the three girls?"

"Yes, sir, that's correct. There were also a few incidents where I had my brother and my nephew watch the girls to make sure they were all right, for my sake. I knew they were the only family Sophie had. I wish that they would've told Mandy what they were doing."

"So you cared about the girls enough to see how they were but you didn't go see them? Did Sophie call or visit them?"

"No, sir, she didn't. I had told her I didn't want children, and she couldn't have any, which might be one reason she was so protective of her nieces. They lived a couple of hours away, and Sophie was a nurse; she always worked. There was one time when I thought she snuck over there to see them, but I never found out, and now I never will, but I do hope for everyone's sake that she got to see them one last time."

There was a long pause before Sheriff Ziree asked, "Is there anything else?"

"Yes, sir. Sorry. My wife's passing is very hard for me, and reliving all this makes me sick to my stomach."

"I understand, but please continue."

"So as I've said, my brother and nephew had watched them. When my wife died, I called my cousin. He was just supposed to get the girls and bring them here. Mandy and her friend—I'm not sure of his name—refused to let the girls leave with my cousin. He was a stranger who was related to me, so I understood. And I didn't want my cousin to tell them Sophie died, so I guess Mandy had it in her head that I just wanted to hurt the girls. I never would've hurt them; I just used them as a scare tactic to get Sophie to do what I wanted. I told my cousin to tell Mandy whatever he needed to in order to scare her. What he told her, I have no idea.

"Eventually, I received a call saying he got the girls and that they were on their way. I waited patiently for them. I received a call twenty minutes later from my cousin, saying that the girls had to go to the bathroom, so they stopped at a gas station. He then told me that Mandy and the guy followed them and took the girls back—I'm guessing through the back door of the bathroom. I told him to get the girls back and I would give him a bonus; I was already going to pay him for picking them up for me. We hung up.

"He called a little later and said there had been an accident. He said he had the girls and they were passed out in the back seat of his car. He told me he got the girls out and into his car and that the car Mandy and her friend were in exploded. He took the girls to the hospital, and I rushed up there. I knew they wouldn't want to see me, but I needed to see them, to make sure they were okay, and I wanted to bring them back here. As I was in the waiting room at the hospital, I heard and saw the news about Mandy and her friend dying in the car. I brought the girls to Sophie's house and tried to tell Amber that Sophie and Mandy were both dead, but she's just a kid; she doesn't want to believe it."

"Mr. Vince, I'm going to need you to write down the names of everyone in your family who you had spy on or interact with Mandy and the nieces. Also, on a different paper, write down what you just told me. Then sign and date it. Now, from what you've said, your nephew is the only one who actually physically hurt people. Is that correct?"

"Yes, it is. Sir, I'm not hiding anything. You can put me away for as long as you'd like. When my wife died, I felt as if I did too."

"Well, I do appreciate your being honest with me and coming in. Also, thank you for bringing the girls here. They will be safe. You will be facing time, but I'm not sure how much. That all depends on the judge. Now please stand so I can read you your rights and put your hands behind your back."

Harvey did as he was told and said he didn't need a lawyer. He walked to the cell, and Sheriff Ziree told the girls they would have to go somewhere else for a while.

CHAPTER 17

ORPHANAGE

A few hours later, the girls were taken to an orphanage. They went to their room and met with a caseworker while the sheriff went to talk to the director, Lucy, and tell her about them. "These girls have been through literal hell and back … and back again. I can assure you, though, that no one will ever come here and hurt anyone. The men who did these things to the girls are behind bars. I have this written list of names." He handed her the list. "These people are related to Harvey, the man who is responsible for the girls' misery, and he is not, under any circumstances, allowed to see these girls or know they're here. As I've said, I highly doubt anything will occur, but just in case …

"I also provided the names of their biological parents, who are behind bars and are not allowed, under any circumstances, to have them. All the biological family I could find are included on the list. If any of the biological family members do come to get the girls, I want to be notified immediately, and I want to be here the day they leave with them. I will call every now and then to check on them. If the girls need anything at all, please do not hesitate to call me." He handed her his card. "And please notify me if they get adopted out."

"Sir, these girls have had quite a life. Will they be okay with random people coming in to observe? Or even if they do get adopted out, will they be all right with complete strangers taking them away, whether it be to a different city or state?" Lucy, the director, was shocked about the girls' story and felt for them.

"In all honesty, ma'am, I'm not sure. It may take them awhile to trust you or the other staff here. If it's okay with you, I would like to call a counselor to come meet with the girls. Maybe a couple of times a week to start and eventually they should be, um, all right. It could take a while before the girls are actually fine. The twins are younger, so they may not remember as much as Amber."

"Yes, sir. We actually know of a counselor; her name is Julie Bee. Here's her card if you would like to talk to her about the girls' case. Do you remember the Griffin murder?"

"Yes, ma'am. That was a couple of counties over, wasn't it?"

"Yes. There was a survivor, their four-year-old daughter, Teresa. She didn't have any living family, and the sheriff brought her to us. From what the little girl told me, she was hiding in her closet. She came down when the noise stopped and saw her mom, dad, and older brother dead in the kitchen, where they'd all been getting dinner ready. Anyway, Ms. Bee comes and sees her and she's getting better day by day." Lucy grabbed some tissues and wiped her eyes. "If you'll also allow Julie to come meet with the girls, I can make their schedule different from the other little girls."

"The world we live in now is sad. I heard they did catch the man who did that though. I assume you will tell the rest of the staff about these three? I don't want the staff to treat them any different, but they have to try to understand just how much these girls have been through and how they may not act like normal children of their age. Will the three be in separate rooms? They're used to being together. They have had social interaction with other kids at school, but they may be heavily guarded."

"They will be in the same room as kids their age, and I can arrange for them to sleep next to each other."

"That would be perfect. In addition, the twins are turning five in a week and a half, on the ninth. Will you give them something for me?"

"Of course."

"It's in my car. I'll be right back." He went out to his car and returned with an envelope on top of two Build-A-Bear Workshop boxes. "These are a couple of stuffed animals that their aunt Sophie had gotten them; she was hoping to see them on their birthday. And this"—he pulled out a second envelope and a small jewelry box—"is for Amber's birthday on July twenty-fourth. It was her aunt Sophie's, so please make sure she takes good care of it."

"Not a problem. I'll let the cafeteria know as well so we can bake them a special birthday cake; we like to do that for those whose birthdays we know."

"Thank you so much for taking the girls. I know they'll be perfect here. I'll just go say my goodbyes and get back to the station."

"Sure, go right ahead."

Sheriff Ziree went and said his goodbyes to the girls, who didn't want him to leave. "Sheriff Ziree, why can't we go back to Aunt Sophie's house? We can live there." Amber had tears in her eyes. All the adults she loved were either dead or in jail. The poor girls had been through way too much.

"Who would watch you, silly?"

"I would. I can watch Emmy and Maddie all by myself. And you can come live with us."

The sheriff almost teared up when he observed the sadness in her eyes. "Amber, I have a family. I have my wife and a little boy and girl. We just can't do that. I'm sorry. You'll be safe here with Emily and Ms. Rose, your teacher. They'll take way better care of you. You wouldn't want to live with me anyway. I'm always at work; I wouldn't have time to play with you three. Look over there. See? Your sisters are already playing." He smiled, trying to reassure her that everything was going to be fine.

"But I don't like having all these new kids here with us." Sheriff Ziree chuckled at that. "Look, I promise you that you and your sisters will get out of here and live amazing lives. But you have to promise me something, that you three will come visit me when you do."

"All right." Amber was still sad, but once she saw her sisters playing and laughing, she felt a little better.

"Come here. Give me a hug." Sheriff Ziree gave Amber a big bear hug and then went over to the twins, giving them hugs before waving goodbye and leaving.

The orphanage was big, with about forty or fifty children ranging from a couple of months to fifteen years old. There were a few over fifteen, but Lucy thought they probably wouldn't get adopted out, so she had them work there to earn money. They helped in the kitchen and the children's rooms. They had seven rooms and six bathrooms, including a nursery. All ages were separated. Ages newborn to two were in one room, two to five in another, five to nine in another, and ten to fifteen in another. The remaining rooms were used for sleeping, and there was a bathroom in every room but the nursery. There was a certain staff member for every room, plus Lucy. They had "school" every other day, where volunteers would come in and teach the children from ages nine to twelve. The girls were put in the five-to-nine room with about seventeen other children.

For the first few days, the girls preferred to play by themselves, and after Lucy explained their situation to Ms. Rose, their teacher, she understood why. A few kids had introduced themselves, but Ms. Rose didn't want to push the girls into interacting.

After another few days went by, the girls opened up a little. They started introducing themselves and playing together. Amber didn't leave her sisters' sides except to go to the bathroom.

On the twins' birthday, after they had lunch, Lucy handed the twins their boxes and the envelope. They opened the boxes to find the cutest little bears they'd ever seen. The twins hugged their bears, and they heard their aunt's voice saying, "Happy birthday, Maddie! I love you so much! *Muahahaha!*" and "Happy birthday, Em! I love you so much! *Muahahahh!*" Inside the envelope was a note:

> Madison and Emily, you girls are so smart, so beautiful, and so brave. I love you two and Amber so much, and I hate that you had to go away. Never forget that so many people love you three girls. I'll see you soon, I promise. I love you girls.
>
> Love, Sophie

Principal Taylor and the entire police station had also signed it. The girls were now crying. Lucy allowed the girls to go into her office and have some privacy.

She called Sheriff Ziree and told him she had given the twins their birthday gifts, adding how much they loved them. An hour later, they were okay, and went to play with a few friends and their bears.

The counselor came in to meet the girls for the first time. "Hi, you must be Amber. I'm Julie," she said. She was an attractive woman in her midthirties, with black hair and a kind smile.

"Hi. These are my sisters, Madison and Emily."

They went into the sleeping room to talk while the other kids played next door. "I heard that you three are very special," Julie said.

"How?" asked Amber.

"Well, I've heard you have been through a lot, and that makes you three super special, like super girls."

"Wow. But we don't have superpowers."

"Oh, but you do. You three have super hearts and super brains. I've been told you three are super smart and brave."

"That's what everyone says, but we're not."

"Amber, I think you are. Anyway, well, I just came in to meet you three and say hi. May I come back the day after tomorrow and talk to you?"

"Okay."

"All right. Let's get you back with your friends."

The girls went back into their room to play, and Julie went to talk to Lucy about the girls. "Amber talked to me; the twins didn't. I'm guessing Amber always does the talking when it comes to the girls. What I would like to do is separate the twins from Amber to see if they would open up and communicate. Amber is really sweet, but she acts depressed and guarded, and someone her age shouldn't act that way; it may cause problems in the future."

"I have noticed Amber's always talking for them. The twins *will* talk to Ms. Rose about simple things, like asking for water or having to go to the bathroom. If Amber doesn't get the counseling she needs, what do you think will happen?" Lucy was worried that Amber may do something drastic later on in life.

"Well, some people turn to drugs, alcohol, crime, or suicide—I'm not saying Amber will. She is very bright and aware for her age. She is, however, used to the crime, drugs, and alcohol already, from what Sheriff Ziree has told me, and that's pretty much all she knows."

"Yes, that's all they all know. I want you to do your best with these girls. Do you think the twins may have a better chance of forgetting and possibly opening up and having a better life?"

"I honestly hope so. I'm afraid we'll just have to wait and see though. If it's all right with you, I would like to stand in and be their teacher as well as their counselor. They've been in school before, but they need one-on-one time and special attention." The two women stood up and shook hands.

Two days later, Julie came back to speak with the girls. "Hello, girls. Can I see you three in here for a minute?" Julie and the girls went to the sleeping room. "How are you all today?"

Amber spoke up. "We're good."

"Glad to hear it."

They all sat at the table, and Julie pulled a coloring book and crayons out of her bag. "Can you three do me a big favor and color me a picture?"

"Sure." Amber was beaming. She loved coloring.

"Thank you. Here, I'm going to let you all choose one." She

ripped out a few pages and had them choose which ones they wanted. They all started coloring their own pages, and Julie was thinking about how to get Emily and Madison to talk more; she didn't want to separate them quite yet. "So, Amber, have you made any friends?"

"My sisters are my friends. I don't need anybody else."

"Amber, everybody needs friends. How about you, Emily? Do you have any friends?"

"I have Amber, Maddie, Ms. Rose, you, and Wendy."

"Who's Wendy?"

"My bear Aunt Sophie got me." She showed her the bear. Ms. Rose, Lucy, and Julie had all decided it was best that the girls had their bears, for a little while at least.

"Oh, okay. Good. What about you, Madison?"

"I have Amber, Em, Lucy, you, Ms. Rose, Ginger, and Gracie."

"Is Ginger your bear?"

"Yes."

"Who's Gracie?"

"She's a girl in our room; she's really nice. She lets me play with her."

"Madison, have Amber and Emily met her?"

Maddison nodded.

"Can I meet her?"

"Sure."

Julie stood up to go into the other room. "You girls keep coloring your pictures for me; I'll be right back." She went to ask Ms. Rose if she could borrow Gracie.

"Sure. But why do you need Gracie?"

"I think she and Madison are her friends, and I would love for the other girls to get acquainted and be her friend as well."

"Oh. Gracie sweetie, can you go with Julie for a minute?"

"Sure." Gracie stood up and went with Julie to the sleeping room. Gracie was a six-year-old who had been in the orphanage since she was about two.

"Hi, Gracie." Madison instantly had a smile on her face.

"Hi, Madison. What are you coloring?" Gracie went over and sat by Madison, and Julie gave her a coloring page.

"I'm coloring a princess." Madison cheered and showed off her picture.

"Hi, Gracie. I'm Julie. I hear you and Madison are friends."

"Yes. She's my best friend." Gracie smiled.

"That's sweet, Gracie. Have you met Amber and Emily?"

"Yes, I met them the first day, and I've seen them play. They play with each other, away from everybody else."

"Well, I was hoping that the four of you could be friends. You've been here a while, haven't you, Gracie?"

"Yes, since I was a baby in Cheryl's room—that's what Ms. Rose tells me."

"So you know a lot of kids, don't you, Gracie?"

"Yes. I know everybody in my class … and some older kids too. They're nice."

"Amber, Gracie seems nice. Could you play with her and be her friend?" Amber just shrugged her shoulders.

"Gracie, would you like to be friends with Amber?"

"Sure, I like making friends."

"What about you, Emily? Will you be friends with Gracie?"

"Sure. If Maddie likes her, I can too." Emily smiled at Gracie.

"Great! I love to hear that. Are we done coloring now?"

"Yes," they all said at the same time, giving Julie their papers. She had written their names on the papers so she could keep them in her folder.

"You three did very well. Many pretty colors. Okay, I won't

keep you much longer. So next time I come back, I would love to hear about how all of you are playing together and being nice to each other."

They all nodded, the twins and Gracie smiling and Amber still not sure. "Today's Thursday. I'll be here Monday to see you again. Now, let's get you all back to your room."

When Monday arrived, true to her word, Julie came back. The girls were eating lunch, and Julie went to talk to Lucy. "Hello, how are you doing today?" Julie asked as she entered Lucy's office.

"I'm doing fine. How are you?"

"I'm good. I came to talk about Amber and her sisters."

"I've noticed they've taken a liking to Gracie; she's such a sweet girl."

"I understand she's been here awhile. How long, exactly?"

"Gracie was brought to us when she was just under two."

"Oh, wow. If you had to guess, how long would you say children stay here on average before getting adopted out?"

"That all depends on who's adopting, whether they want a baby or a child and if that child and that adult have a bond."

"Okay. So on average, about how long would Amber and her sisters be in here?"

"That's a hard case considering most people adopting want a baby and/or just one child. Amber and her sisters make three. It's rare that siblings are adopted together—and triple that for three. At one point, we had four siblings up here, ranging from five to fourteen. All but the fourteen-year-old were adopted, and only two stayed together. We encourage their new parents to stay in contact with the other siblings and parents. We even allow them to call up here. Sadly, that doesn't always happen."

"So, for instance, if the twins were adopted out without Amber, would you still allow them to come visit her and play with her?"

"Oh, absolutely. We would allow Amber and her sisters, weather permitting, to go outside and play, and I would have one of the older kids keep watch."

"In my honest opinion, I don't think any of them should be put up for adoption yet. Granted, it may take months for them to get adopted, but it may also take days. I'm here to make sure that, if separated, the girls will be all right and will also be able to see and/or contact each other. As of right now, I can tell you that the twins are okay without Amber, especially Emily. So my next goal—but not today—is to separate Amber and Emily somehow.

Madison's more independent; I would say about thirty percent more. She's still guarded, but she has opened a little more, and she said she was playing with Gracie a week ago versus the other two, who were playing by themselves in a corner. I'm about to go speak with them now; I was waiting on them to finish lunch."

"I've noticed Madison does seem to speak more than the other two."

"She does. They should be done with lunch now. I'll just see my way to their room." She left Lucy's office and went into the girls' room to talk to them.

A couple of hours later, she walked out, happy that they had a good session. She returned to Lucy's office and took a seat. "I'm really happy to announce that the girls are now friends with three of the other children. Emily opened up a little, which is amazing. We had a good session."

"Oh, good. I'm so glad!"

"I'll be back in tomorrow to talk to Teresa. I'll see you then."

After Julie left, Lucy called Sheriff Ziree to let him know how well the girls were doing.

CHAPTER 18
BIRTHDAY SURPRISE

Two months had passed, and it was very successful as far as the girls' socialization was going. Julie, Ms. Rose, and Lucy were proud of how far they had come in just a short couple of months.

"I think the girls are ready to be put up for adoption. As we've mentioned before, it could take weeks, months even." Lucy was bringing this to Julie's attention.

"They have come so far in these past two months. I'm so happy I can have conversations with all of them now, not just Amber. They are very happy here, but I do agree with you that it could take months. These girls are too precious not to have parents who love them. I will miss them terribly when they do go." Julie would be sad, but she also believed all children needed parents who would love and protect them.

"Do you think they will be fine if they can't stay together? I will do everything in my power to persuade the parents to take all three, but sometimes it's one, two, or none. I know it would break their hearts being apart, but as I've mentioned before, I do allow them to see and contact each other." Lucy was sure they would be fine eventually, but she wanted Julie's professional opinion.

"The twins were so young when all this happened that they may actually forget a little, and if they could possibly stay together, that would be better. Amber, though, was six when all this started, so she'll have memory of it. She may forget little details, but she won't completely forget. I want them all to stay together, but we have to think of the worst possible scenario, that being they all get separated. If this happens, especially in Amber's case, she could suffer from depression and separation anxiety. The other two could definitely have some issues as well, but Amber is older and more aware. We need to let the new guardians know of their situation, which is why I would advise you to give the girls' new guardians my personal cell number, as well as Sheriff Ziree's. He's seen these girls in the best and worst places in their lives. He would relate more on an emotional level exactly what they've been through."

"I'll get these papers filed so that they'll be able to get adopted. I'll make sure Ms. Rose is aware of this. Usually when new parents come in, they ask to see children of certain ages, newborn up to two, five up to seven, something like that. Other parents just go to the rooms and have an instant connection with the children. If parents do ask to see children, say, three to five years old, I would have to allow them to see Madison and Emily, and if they are chosen, I would let the parents know about Amber, and vice versa with Amber. Usually parents choose a child, and I like to give them time with the child to get to know them, so I allow them to go outside and play, with me watching, or in the sleeping room, again with me watching. Regarding the twins, it's possible they'd stay together—new parents usually love twins, and let's face it, they're adorable."

"Yes, let's hope the twins stay together, for their own sake.

And let's hope if the parents don't take Amber, her new parents will allow the girls to stay in contact."

"All right. Let me get this done and I'll have to go see to it that the children have lunch." They both stood.

"I do feel the girls will only need to see me one day a week now, and of course there's Teresa. So my new schedule will consist of coming Monday for Teresa and Thursday for them."

"That sounds good. We will see you Monday. Have a good afternoon."

A week later, Julie came back to see the girls. "Hello, Amber, Madison, and Emily. Are you three ready to go play outside?" It was nice out.

"Yeah!"

"I'll go get some water and spray, and then we'll all go out."

Julie took them all out to the playground, where they ran off in separate directions. She was observing their new independent behavior. The twins no longer needed to be next to Amber, and vice versa. The sisters did love playing together, but they were their own individual selves and needed their own time to figure out what they liked separately.

While they were outside, a couple pulled into the parking lot and went inside. *Oh no, this could be it,* Julie was thinking. Ever since her conversation with Lucy the prior week, the girls being separated was all she'd been thinking about.

The couple had been inside for forty minutes when Julie decided to take the girls inside. As they started to walk out the gate, Lucy showed up with the couple and Gracie. "Hi, Gracie!" the girls said. They started talking among themselves.

"My apologies, Julie. I forgot you four were out here."

"Oh, that's quite all right. We were just heading inside. Hello, Gracie."

"Hi."

"Is this your big day?"

"I hope so." She smiled and then went to play.

"Come on, girls. Let's head inside."

Julie took the girls back inside and went to talk to Ms. Rose.

"Is Gracie getting adopted?"

"I hope so. That poor girl's been here for a little over four years. If anyone deserves this, it's her."

"Julie," Amber interrupted.

"What's up, sweetie?"

"Is Gracie going to go away?" She looked sad.

Julie sat in a chair and held Amber's hands. "She may get adopted. But hey, don't be sad. She's going to have a brand-new mommy and daddy, and they are going to love her so much. She'll probably have her own room, and they'll probably go to fun places and have good times together."

"I want a new mommy and daddy too, with Maddie and Em."

"You three will have new mommies and daddies soon, I'm sure."

"Okay." Amber left, likely unaware that Julie had just said "mommies and daddies," as in plural.

"We have to explain to children every time their friends get adopted out, and it makes them sad, so we have to tell them not to cry or worry and tell them almost exactly what you told Amber." Ms. Rose was trying to make Julie feel better. "You didn't lie to her. You just made it look better. I'm sure in any child's mind, any house and parents are a fairy tale compared to here."

"I guess you're right. I have to go, but when you know if Gracie is getting adopted, will you call me? I need to make sure Amber and her sisters are all right with it. They've had so many people come and go."

"I absolutely will."

"Thank you."

Julie received a call an hour later from Ms. Rose, saying Gracie was adopted out and the girls were taking it surprisingly well after Ms. Rose told them Gracie was going to live with her new mom and dad.

"Great. Thanks for the call." Julie was thankful that the girls were fine and that it didn't upset them or set them back.

A week and a half later, the girls still missed their best friend, but they knew she was happier with her new family.

Amber's birthday was in three days, and her whole room was excited. Ms. Rose kept a big calendar on the wall with all the kids' birthdays. She told everyone that they were going to sing "Happy Birthday" and have cake and ice cream.

Amber was playing with her friends Gabriel and Olivia when Lucy came in the room. She went over to talk to Ms. Rose and then went out and called Sheriff Ziree.

"Hey, Lucy. What's going on?" he asked. "Are the girls all right?"

"Yes, they're fine," Lucy said. "I got a call thirty minutes ago from a Mrs. Weather, asking to meet her granddaughters. I saw on the file that Weather is their mom's maiden name."

"Their mother had no contact with her mother that I knew of. Amber's parents are still in prison, unless somehow she called or the mother went up there. Even then, the prison is heavily guarded. Can you give me the number?"

"Certainly."

He wrote the number down as she gave it. "Thank you. I'm going to call and have them meet me here at the station. If she is Amber's grandma, I may allow her to come meet the girls. Would that be okay?"

"Yes."

"Okay. I'll call you back and let you know."

"Thank you so much."

He called back in an hour and told her that the woman was indeed the girls' grandma and he was allowing them to meet. "She will follow me to the orphanage. We'll be there in forty-five minutes or so. Please have the girls out of their room by then."

"Will do, sir. Thank you. See you then."

Thirty-five minutes later, she went and got the girls. "Hey, girls, come on in here." Lucy led the girls into her office.

"What is it?" Amber asked.

"Sheriff Ziree has someone he wants you to meet. He's on his way now."

"Sheriff Ziree's coming?" Amber was clearly excited now.

"Yes, he'll be here anytime. Can you three play in here until he gets here?"

"Yes," all three of them answered.

They played for a few minutes, and then Sheriff Ziree walked through the door. "Mr. Ziree!" Amber and her sisters all jumped in his arms.

"Hi, girls! I heard you're doing great here. Are you having fun?"

They all nodded happily.

"That's wonderful. It makes me very happy."

"Why are you here? Who's with you?" Amber asked, trying to look outside. "Amber, I know you were sad when your mommy and daddy went away, right?"

"Yeah, it was sad."

"Your grandma, your mom's mom, contacted Lucy, who then contacted me. Amber, Madison, and Emily, would you like to meet your grandma?"

"Grandma? Mommy told me when I was little that I didn't have a grandma." Amber was confused and a little excited.

"You do have a grandma."

Amber gasped in excitement. She had heard stories about grandparents spoiling their grandchildren. "Is she here to take us home?" Amber was beyond excited now.

"Sweetheart, calm down." Sheriff Ziree chuckled and opened the door for them. "Mrs. Weather, this is Amber, Emily, and Madison. Girls, this is your grandma."

Mrs. Weather smiled down at them. "Hello, girls. I'm Mary. I'm your mom's mom."

"Hi!" they all three said at once.

"You girls are so cute. You get that from me." She smiled and winked at them.

"Did you talk to my mommy and daddy?" Amber asked her.

"Yes, I talked to your mommy. She said she loves you and misses you."

"Yay. I love her and miss her too."

"I'm sure you do, sweetie."

"Mrs. Weather, can I speak with you for just a minute?" Sheriff Ziree asked her.

"Sure."

"Girls, will you three play in here for just a minute? Lucy, do you mind?"

"Not at all. Take your time."

"Mrs. Weather, as I explained to you at the police station, you can bring up her parents—that's fine—but don't go getting their hopes up as far as them going back to live there. I've told you both about what your daughter and her husband did. Amber and her sisters are very happy here. They just got their lives back on track, and I cannot be having their past come back to haunt them, not saying you would ever let that happen again. Now, because of how your daughter was around the girls, she and her husband are not allowed custody of the girls. You have never met the girls, right?"

"That's true. I received a call from the prison, and I was in shock. I had no idea who it could be. When Ashlyn was a junior in high school, she started acting out. She moved out and lived with her fiancé. I wasn't sure if they actually got married, but I guess they did at one point.

So anyway, I answered the phone and it was Ashlyn. She said she was in prison and only had a few minutes to talk. She said they had three little girls. She said they'd be five and eight by now and we should have the right to know them. I went to the prison to talk to her, and she didn't know where the girls ended up. She told us maybe the Deras, but I called the police station and learned they had passed. I tried to contact Sophie, who was very sickly, to see if maybe she knew them, and she said she had them but she was too sick now so her friend had them. I then saw the wreck on the news, about the car exploding, and I didn't really think anything of it until now. I then looked for the last resort, the internet. I looked up orphanages around here, and this orphanage popped up. I clicked on the website and saw a picture of three sisters that needed to be adopted, ages five and seven. I called up here, and the director said she would have to call me back, but I guess she contacted you … and you contacted me. I never knew they existed until maybe five months ago."

"They've been here for four months now. They have had to go through some therapy and now act and play like five- and seven-year-olds should. They used to be so guarded. Amber was depressed at one time. Amber will be eight on the twenty-fourth. They have been through so much, as I'm sure you're aware."

"I've heard all about what they've been through. Will I be able to take them home with me?"

"Ma'am, I'm sad to say they cannot. Even if I do monitor you and the girls, if by some chance their parents get out, it would make it easier for their parents to find them. I'm not meaning to be rude; I'm just thinking about what's best for the girls. I let you come meet them because I do believe the girls should know some of their family, not just the bad parts of their parents or what happened to Sophie. I promise that after they are adopted out, I will make it my duty to call you and tell you—also ask their new parents if they will allow for visitation, supervised, of course. After the girls become of age, I can't make rules. If they wish to have a relationship with you, or their parents, they can."

"Will they be separated?"

"Ma'am, I honestly don't know. I have asked Lucy, and she says that it's very rare for three siblings to get adopted out together. She said the twins might stay together, if any, but she will do her best and try to persuade the new parents to take all three. As I've said, they are doing much better now. I call up here every so often, and Lucy tells me that they are beginning to act and play like kids their age should."

"I'm really happy that you let me meet them. I wish we could bring them home, love on them, and keep them safe. They are all beautiful girls. Am I allowed to go tell Ashlyn that they're safe and happy? Or is that allowed?"

"You may tell her that the girls are happy now and that when they become of age, if they wish to have that contact with their parents, they can. You can tell them that the girls cannot come live with the two of you under the circumstances. You can't tell them where the girls are or who their new parents are when they do get adopted. Pretty much just stick to saying that the girls are safe and happy now, they are not allowed to come stay with you, and when they are of age, they can decide what they want to do."

"Yes, sir. Thank you. Can we go say goodbye to the girls now?"

"Absolutely."

They went back in to see the girls. "It was so wonderful to meet you three. You're all very special."

"Can we come home with you, Grandma?" Amber asked, hopeful. Her grandma got a little tear in her eye when Amber called her that.

"Amber," Sheriff Ziree butted in, "I brought your grandma to come meet you and your sisters because she deserves to know the amazing girls that you three are. Do you remember Mr. and Mrs. Dera and how you had to go away because they were too old to care for you three?"

"Yes." Amber remembered and was sad at the memories.

"Well, the same thing with your grandma, but I promise you that you and your sisters will have a new mommy and daddy who love you very much and nothing will ever hurt you. You can see your grandma later. Can you three give her a hug?"

The girls said their goodbyes and gave big bear hugs.

"Bye, dears. I'll see you later," Mrs. Weather walked out, got in her car, and drove off.

"Okay, girls, back to Ms. Rose's class," Lucy said after they watched their newly found grandma drive off.

"Bye, Sheriff Ziree," the sisters said.

"Bye girls. Big bear hug?"

The girls all gave hugs and went to their room to have lunch.

"Sir, if she comes back, should I notify you? Are the girls allowed to visit with her?"

"They can visit; I will definitely want to be notified though. I will set a time limit of two hours. That gives enough time for visitation. I will call and notify her of these rules. I will also need to go over the importance of not notifying the girls' mother of their whereabouts. So I'll head back to give them the call."

"Thank you, sir. I will let you know if something else happens."

Sheriff Ziree left, and Lucy fell into her chair. It had been a long day.

Three days later, Amber's room woke up and went to eat breakfast. All the children were saying happy birthday to her when Ms. Rose walked in with pancakes. "Happy birthday, sweetie."

"Thank you." Amber was loving the attention on her birthday.

"Okay, girls, eat up and we'll go out and play today."

"Yay!"

As the girls ate, Ms. Rose went and got cups and water to bring outside with them. "Okay, girls," Ms. Rose said as they were getting in line to go outside, "remember that we have to stay hydrated and drink plenty of water. I put your names on the cup that you will use. Also, for those of you who don't know, this is Ms. Zoe Bird; she will be my helper today. So if I'm unavailable and something happens, she can help." Zoe was one of the oldest teenagers in the orphanage. She was seventeen and would be kicked out soon. They all went outside to have fun.

Lucy came out fifteen minutes later with a couple. "Hi, Ms. Rose. This is Mr. and Mrs. Free; they recently got married, and they are here to adopt a child. They prefer a child who is around the five and nine range. They said the younger the better, but they would just like to see who they have a connection with, if any." She turned to the couple.

"Mr. and Mrs. Free, these are our five- to nine-year-old children. We do have some siblings here. Have you two talked about the possibility of siblings?"

"We have, yes," Mrs. Free said. "We would prefer that the siblings were either the same age or only a little bit apart in age, and we couldn't do with more than two. We only have two spare bedrooms we could use for them, if we do take that route."

"All right. I'll let you two go introduce yourselves. I hope today is someone's lucky day. Ms. Rose will be here—she's the teacher for this room—and that's Zoe over there; she's also an orphan but also a helper. She knows about a few of these children but not all."

"Okay, thank you," Mr. Free said as they looked among the children. They walked around and watched the children playing, and a few walked up to them and introduced themselves.

"These children are very sweet," Mrs. Free said as they walked around. "It's sad that they get put up for adoption."

"Some don't have a choice, dear. Some parents give them up because they simply can't afford to take care of them."

"That's true. Look how cute she is." She pointed over to Amber playing on the slide.

"She's adorable. Let's go introduce ourselves," her husband said.

"Hi," Mrs. Free said as they approached. "I'm Tammy, and this is Daniel. What's your name?"

"I'm Amber."

"Do you like playing on the slide?"

"Yes, it's fun." She smiled and slid down the slide. "Whee!"

When Ms. Rose noticed that Mr. and Mrs. Free were talking to Amber, she grew nervous. She looked over at Amber's sisters, who were playing together, oblivious to the situation. She then noticed the couple coming back to where she was.

"Hello. The little girl over on the slide is very cute. How old is she? Does she have any siblings?"

"That's Amber. She's been here since the end of March. Today's her birthday. She's eight. She does have two other siblings here." She pointed to Emily and Madison. "The set of twins, Emily and Madison, are five."

"They're adorable too. All these kids are beautiful. As we've said, we'll take up to two siblings, but three's too many for us to deal with right now. I really don't want to separate them. We'll keep looking. If we don't find anyone else, do you think it would be possible to have Amber without her sisters?"

"It is possible, yes. However, you may want to talk to Lucy about separating them and coming to visit. If you are interested in knowing their background, Lucy has to be the one to tell you. Amber is very sweet and smart, but we do have other children who are equally as sweet and smart."

"All right, we'll just watch for a few more minutes and discuss it."

"Yes, ma'am. Take your time. We'll be out here another"— she looked at her watch—"fifteen minutes. It's kind of hot."

"Yes, ma'am."

Mr. and Mrs. Free walked around the playground again and tried to talk to a few more children, but Mrs. Free was still drawn to Amber for some reason. When the fifteen minutes were up, Ms. Rose told the children to get in line. She did a head count while Zoe walked across the playground, and they all went inside. Mr. and Mrs. Free followed and went in to see Lucy.

Lucy welcomed them into her office and sat behind her desk. "Hello. I hope the children had good behavior while you observed."

"Yes, they're all splendid," Mrs. Free said as her and her husband sat down.

"That's wonderful. Have you two made any connection with any? Or made a decision?"

"Ma'am, we were wondering if you could tell us about Amber."

"Amber? Oh, she's wonderful. Such a sweetheart, as are her sisters."

"They are really sweet. For some reason, I feel a connection with Amber. My husband and I have talked to other children out there, but I feel I'm being drawn to her somehow."

"Okay. Are you aware she has twin sisters?"

"Yes, I am. I honestly would hate to tear them apart. Do you mind if we go home and think this over? We'll give you a call as soon as we've made up our minds."

"Sure." They all stood and shook hands. "Thank you two so much for coming."

They headed for the door. "No problem. We will let you know as soon as we've made our decision."

"You two have a good day." She waved as she stood in her doorway.

A few days later, Lucy received a call from Mrs. Free. "Hello. Lucy, my husband's at work right now, but I was wondering if I could come by."

"No problem. Have you made a decision?"

"My husband and I have. Can I come up there and discuss it? I can be there in twenty minutes."

"Sure. I'll see you then."

Oh, please don't separate these girls, Lucy thought.

Thirty minutes later, Mrs. Free walked in. "Hello, Mrs. Free. How are you today?"

"I'm good. How are you?"

"I'm doing well. So let's get down to it," she said as they sat down. "Have you two made your decision?"

"We have, but I have some questions."

"Of course. Which child is this regarding?"

"Amber."

"Let me get her file and we'll start." As she was locating her file, she started sweating a puddle (at least that's what it felt like). "Here it is. Amber is a very special little girl who's been through way too much. What kind of questions did you have?"

"Regarding her sisters, if we do adopt Amber, do you think her sisters will fall into some type of separation anxiety or depression?"

"With that, it is a possibility. We actually have had a therapist come in and talk to these girls. Why don't I give her a call and see if she's available? Just one second."

"All right, sounds good."

She hung up the phone after a few minutes and turned to Mrs. Free. "She said she can be here in fifteen minutes. Can I answer any other questions while we wait?"

"Sure. Were their parents abusive in any way?"

"Their parents neglected the children, but as far as I've heard, they've never been abused, at least not physically. She went to the hospital when she was six because she lived in a home where her parents smoke, drank, did drugs, and so forth, and she had an excessive amount of smoke in her lungs. The sheriff on that case actually calls and comes up here every once in a while and checks on them. If you can wait about thirty minutes, I can possibly get him up here too."

"That would be perfect. I'm just trying to see the best option, if there is one, where we can adopt Amber and she'll be fine."

"Just one second. Let me give him a call."

"He said he can be here in thirty minutes. Is that all right?" Lucy asked her a few minutes later.

"Yes, that's fine."

"See you then, sir. Bye."

The two women were talking for a few more minutes when Julie knocked on the door. "Come on in," Lucy said as she stood.

"Hello, Lucy. And you must be Mrs. Free." Julie shook both women's hands and sat down.

"Thank you for coming Julie. Mrs. Free is interested in Amber and was wondering if you think it would be okay to just take her and not both of her siblings. She was wondering if Amber's sisters would have some type of separation anxiety or depression."

Julie looked at Mrs. Free, who looked very interested in what she had to say. "Mrs. Free, I have been here with the girls ever since they arrived, and I can tell you that I am very happy with how fast these girls have adapted in this situation."

"We have Sheriff Ziree coming in to discuss the girls' situation so it's clearer. He'll be in about twenty minutes," Lucy interjected.

"Perfect. He was there, so he'll know more about that. Regarding the depression or separation anxiety you're asking about, the twins definitely talked and opened up more than Amber when I first started seeing them. They had a good friend in here who was adopted out not too long ago. We thought the girls would have a tough time with letting go—and not only letting go per se, more like getting out of the routine of not having their friend there when they wake up, go play, and so on. I'm not saying this is the same by any means, but compared to how they would've handled that before versus now, it's tremendous progress. I come up here to visit a few children, and some I don't even come to see any more because they have gotten better. I don't need to come see these three as much because they are doing so much better in trusting and building friendships with other people. If you decide to take Amber—again, your decision—I would come see the twins more and we would be able to update you on their progress, if you wish."

"As I've told Lucy, I don't want to be the cause of any more problems the girls will have to face."

"We understand completely."

"I'm going to butt in for just one second," Lucy said. "Mrs. Free, I have had other siblings up here who didn't get adopted together. And as sad as it sounds, I don't know if they have a relationship with each other. I do allow siblings to come visit. If you do take Amber, for example, I will give you total permission to bring her to see her sisters. I'll let you go outside, with a teacher, or I'll allow her to stay in the classroom with them. She can also call up here if she just wants to talk to her sisters. If the twins are adopted out, I will also provide the parents with your name and number, if that's okay with you. I try to push parents into keeping siblings in contact."

"Absolutely. I'll let Amber call and come visit when we can. I give you permission to give out my name and number to the twins' new parents. Three girls is a lot to take on; imagine when they're sixteen and thirteen. Teen city." They all laughed a little at that one.

They was another knock on the door; it was Sheriff Ziree. "Hello, Lucy and Julie, and you must be Mrs. Free." He shook all their hands and went to stand by Lucy.

"Thank you for coming, Sheriff. Mrs. Free is interested in

our Amber. We've already answered questions about the twins and whether all the girls will be okay with this change. I've called you in because she was curious about her birth parents and you have dealt with them as well as knew about their other guardian. I've told her about Sophie and her passing and about Mandy and her tragic accident. I'm not sure of any of the details though. We were hoping you could shed some light so Mrs. Free can tell her husband and they will make their decision."

"Certainly. Mrs. Free, I can tell you these girls are special. I love them like my own. On Amber's sixth birthday, Amber was rushed to the hospital. Long story short, her parents were arrested; they aren't allowed contact with them. Their parents are still in prison, and they are allowed supervised visitation—if you allow—when they get out, and when the girls turn eighteen, they can have that relationship if they wish."

He went on to explain how Amber, because she was older, would be more likely to have memories of those moments. "They will be faint because she was six and seven. By the time she's a teen, hopefully she'll forget most of what happened." He looked at Julie. "But that's a Julie question."

"It's a possibility she'll forget; however, most people have flashes of memory, from that age even," Julie confirmed for Sheriff Ziree. "And with the accidents and events being so traumatizing, she'll probably always have flashes. It's sad. Her sisters were only three when she went into the hospital, so they won't remember quite as much. They may have flashes of their aunt and Mandy."

"After they left the hospital, I had them go stay with their elderly neighbors. They were there for almost a year. My paperwork here says ten months. The gentleman got sick, so the wife told me they wouldn't be able to care for the girls anymore. I then got in touch with their aunt, who lived a couple of cities over, and she came as soon as she found out about them. They lived with her for three and a half months. Something happened, and their aunt gave them up to her best friend. Her best friend had them for six months before she had that tragic accident, leaving them orphans. How they came up to my police station is a story for another day, which I will tell you if you're interested. I thought you'd just be okay with the shortened version."

"Wow. They have really bounced from house to house." Mrs. Free was visibly shocked and upset for the girls.

"Yes, they have. I honestly would've taken them in, but I have a family myself, and with my job, I'm always at work. I want the girls to have a happy life with families who love them unconditionally, regardless of their past. I knew the risks in them getting separated when I dropped them off." He said the last part with sadness in his eyes. "That's just how it is."

"As I've said, my husband and I don't want to create any unnecessary trauma for these girls. Lucy, is there any way we could get Amber for maybe a week, just to see how she and her sisters will act without one another? As you said, three siblings rarely are adopted out together. This way, we could try it. If this doesn't work, then we'll go on to another child. I hate to say it like that, but I don't want Amber to be miserable the whole time with us. I will gladly bring her to visit, and she can call whenever she would like." Lucy thought about it for a moment and said, "That actually sounds perfect. We will have to talk to Amber, of course, and ask her what she thinks."

"Oh, I understand."

"All right. Julie, will you go get Amber and bring her in here, please?"

"Sure. I'll be right back."

When she returned with Amber, the little girl ran straight to Sheriff Ziree.

"Hi, Mr. Ziree! What are you doing here? Did you come to see me?"

"Yes, I did, sweetie. Do you remember meeting Mrs. Free?" He knelt down to hug her and pointed at Mrs. Free.

"Yes, she came to see me on the slide. Hi! Where's Mr. Free?"

"Hi, sweetie. He's at work right now; he should be getting off soon though."

"Amber, Mrs. Free has something she wants to ask you, all right?" Sheriff Ziree was nervous himself.

"What is it?" she asked, looking over at Mrs. Free.

"Amber, I was wondering if we could be friends and have a sleepover," Mrs. Free said, very careful with her words.

"Really? Are you going to sleep here?" Amber's eyes grew with excitement.

"How about we go to my house? We can bake cookies, stay up, watch movies, and have popcorn. Does that sound like fun?"

"Yeah. Are Maddie and Em coming too?" She was jumping up and down with pure excitement.

"Sweetie, I was hoping it could just be me, you, and my husband. I'll bring you back tomorrow to see your sisters, I promise."

"I want Maddie and Em to come too," she said, pouting.

"Hey, Amber," Sheriff Ziree interjected, seeing that Mrs. Free didn't know what to say, "how about you go tonight and have this sleepover and I stay here with your sisters and make sure they have a ton of fun too?"

"You'll stay here with them?"

"Sure. I'll make sure they eat and play and you can call and tell them good night."

Amber thought about it for a few minutes and finally said,

"Okay, I'll do it." They all cheered, telling Amber what a good decision she made by herself (even though Sheriff Ziree had helped as far as her sisters were concerned). He wasn't actually going to stay there all night—he couldn't—and he knew it was wrong of him to lie, but he wanted to make this transition easier for everybody, especially the girls.

"Thank you, Amber." Mrs. Free smiled. "Can I have a hug now?"

Amber stepped over and gave Mrs. Free a hug. "Can I go tell Maddie and Em?"

"Julie, will you walk Amber back to her room?" Lucy asked.

"Come on, Amber. This is so exciting. You two are going to have so much fun," she started as they walked out the door.

When they reached Amber's room, Amber ran over to her sisters while Julie went to talk to Ms. Rose.

"You're not going to be here tonight?" Madison asked, her voice sad.

"I'll be back tomorrow though. I need you to promise me to take care of Em."

"Hey, I'm right here. I'm a big girl too!" Emily shouted. The girls laughed before hurrying across the room to play, and Julie looked over from where she was sitting. She wouldn't want that laughter to disappear.

"So is Amber getting adopted for sure or is this just a trial?" Ms. Rose asked, scared of what Julie would say.

"Mrs. Free says she wants to see how Amber and her sisters will react without each other. She says she's formed a bond with Amber. She has offered to take her tonight and bring her back tomorrow. I'll stay here for a couple of hours after Amber leaves so I can keep an eye on the twins."

"Did Amber say she'd go?"

"Yes. It surprised all of us. I am so happy that Amber feels all right with the idea of going somewhere without her sisters. We may have told a little white lie, but it is what's best for her and her sisters. She may call tonight to tell her sisters good night."

"That's great."

"Ms. Rose?" Emily had made her way over to them while the other two continued playing.

"Yes, Emily?"

"Can I let Amber have Wendy tonight? She said she'll be back tomorrow, so she can bring it back."

"Oh, that's so sweet. Go ahead and get it." Smiling, she watched as Emily went into the sleeping room and came out with her bear. She went over to her sisters. "Amber, if I let you borrow Wendy, will you bring her back tomorrow?"

Amber almost started crying because of how sweet her sister was being. She grabbed Emily and hugged her tightly, sandwiching Wendy in between.

"I will take really good care of her."

Julie approached them. "Okay, girls, say goodbye. You'll see each other tomorrow."

CHAPTER 19

THE FREE HOUSE

"**W**ill you get the eggs for me? I forgot them," Mrs. Free said to Amber. It had been a couple of hours, and they were making cookies. Mr. Free had come home and met Amber, again, and they played a little while Mrs. Free got most of the things out for cookies. They were both extremely nice. Mrs. Free was five feet seven, with long brown hair, and she worked as a pharmacist; Mr. Free was five feet ten, with blond hair, and he was a dentist.

"Where are they?"

"Right here." Mrs. Free walked over to the fridge and showed Amber. "Amber, I want you to know you can have whatever's in here to eat or drink. You don't have to be a stranger and ask, okay?"

"All right. Can I have some milk?"

"Sure." Mrs. Free poured Amber some milk, and they went back to mixing the cookie batter.

Mrs. Free showed Amber more of the house while the cookies where baking. "The bathroom's over there, as you've seen. The closet with towels and washcloths is right here. You're more than welcome to take a bath tonight. This is your room …

139

for tonight," Mrs. Free had to catch herself at that last part. "Our bedroom's just right down there if you need anything. And this is our extra bedroom."

"Who stays in there?"

"If someone else comes over, this is usually where they stay."

"So like Maddie and Em?"

"They can come visit after a while; I know you'd love that."

"Yeah! Can they come stay tomorrow?"

"Do *you* want to stay tomorrow?"

"I'm having fun, but I miss Maddie and Em. Are we going to see them tomorrow?"

"Of course we are. Will you come spend tomorrow night too? I don't have work tomorrow, so we can go to the park and go shopping."

"That sounds fun! I want to go see Maddie and Em first though."

"Absolutely. Now, let's go check on those cookies."

They went back to the kitchen, where Mr. Free had taken out the cookies. He was now sitting down watching TV.

"Are they done?" Amber asked him, excited to taste her masterpiece.

"They are, but they have to cool down a bit first." They went into the living room, and he handed her the remote. "Here. Would you like to watch some TV?"

"Do you have *Sophia the First*?" She handed Mr. Free the remote, and he flipped it to the show.

They ate cookies while watching the show for an hour. They all showered, and when Amber was in bed, Mr. and Mrs. Free talked, hoping the transition would be this easy.

The next day, as promised, after they ate and Mr. Free went to work, Mrs. Free took Amber back to the orphanage to see her sisters. Lucy greeted them with a big smile as she opened the door for them. "Good morning! How was the sleepover?"

"It was so fun!" Amber was beaming.

"I'm happy to hear that. Your sisters are in the room playing; you can go join them. Mrs. Free, would you speak with me for a minute?"

"Certainly. Go on, Amber. I'll be in there in a second."

Amber went to her sisters' room, and Lucy and Mrs. Free went in the office. "So how was everything?" Lucy asked. "Obviously, Amber is very happy today, so that's a good sign."

"Last night went by perfectly. She did talk about her sisters, but she knew we were coming back today, so she was fine with it. We baked cookies and watched TV, and she took a bath; she loves that fact that she gets her own bedroom and bathroom unless other people visit. We didn't want anyone coming over and upsetting her or making a big fuss, so we haven't told our families yet. I don't think she realizes we're trying to adopt her. I am ready to make this official. My husband gets off at four, and we can be here at five to sign the papers. Would that be okay?"

"That's perfectly fine. I am so happy to hear that things are going so well. I'm assuming by how ready you are to adopt Amber that she's going with you again tonight?"

"I asked her last night if she would like to spend the night again, and she said yes. She asked me last night about the spare bedroom and if her sisters could come stay. I told her they could eventually. I just hope their new parents accept the fact that they have an older sister and they need each other."

"I will do my best to make that clear to the new parents. I am so happy this worked out so well. I thought Amber would have issues, but I guess we were all worried for no reason. I'll get her paperwork and things together later so when you and your husband come back, everything will be ready."

"All right, thank you so much."

They stood and shook hands. "I'm going to go see Amber and her sisters, if that's okay."

"Well, she's practically yours now." Lucy smiled.

Mrs. Free exited the office and went down to the room, smiling as she entered. "Hello, Ms. Rose. How are you?"

"Hello, Mrs. Free. I'm doing well. Amber told me that she had a great time."

"We all did. Amber, did you tell her what we did?" Amber had walked over and given Mrs. Free a hug.

"We baked cookies! And we watched Sophia."

"It sounds as if you had quite the night. That's awesome to hear!"

"Mrs. Free said we're going to go shopping today!" Amber was jumping up and down with excitement.

"That's really cool. Can I come too?" Ms. Rose chuckled.

"You have to stay here with Maddie and Em."

Ms. Rose looked over at Mrs. Free, who glanced down at Amber and said, "Sweetie, go give Emily her bear back and tell your sisters bye. We're coming back later today."

"Okay." Amber did as she was told, which gave Ms. Rose the perfect opportunity to ask Mrs. Free if they were adopting her.

"Yes. My husband is at work right now, but I told Lucy we would be up here around five to sign the paperwork and get her things. We're going to have a day out today."

"That's wonderful! I love it when children are adopted. I assume you will come up here and visit her sisters?"

"I told Amber that whenever she would like to, we will."

"That's amazing. I'm so happy for all of you."

Amber came back over to them. "Amber, give Ms. Rose a

big hug and tell her we'll be back." Amber did as she was told, and they left for the mall. They walked around and shopped until lunchtime, when they stopped to eat. "So, Amber, what's next?" Mrs. Free asked as they were eating.

"Um ... I don't know."

They continued to eat while Mrs. Free thought about where to go. When they were finished, they got back in the car. "Where are we going?" Amber asked.

"We bought you a new bathing suit, right?"

Amber gave a huge smile. "Are we going swimming?"

"We sure are. We have to go back home, though, so I can get my swimsuit, and then we'll go to the water park."

"Okay!" Amber was excited. Sure, when she lived with Sophie and Mandy, she went swimming in their kiddie pools, and they went swimming when they went to Disney World, but she'd never been to an actual water park, so she was excited. They were at the water park until four, when Mrs. Free told Amber that Mr. Free was off work and would be home soon. They got dried off, changed, and went home to see Mr. Free.

"Hi, Mr. Free!" Amber jumped into his arms.

"Hi, Amber! You know, you can call me Daniel. It's so much easier. Your hair's still wet."

"We went swimming! It was fun!"

"That's good, sweetheart. Want to go watch TV for a few minutes?"

"All right." Amber left the room.

Mr. Free looked at his wife. "Let me change clothes and we'll head to the orphanage."

"Okay."

Forty-five minutes later, they arrived at the orphanage. "Hello again," Lucy said. "Amber, do you want to go see your sisters while we talk?"

"Sure." She went to the room.

"Okay," Lucy said as they entered the office and went to sit, "I got all her paperwork. She had just a couple of things. Is there anything else that you would like to know about Amber before we complete this process?"

"I think we're good," Mr. Free said, and Mrs. Free nodded in agreement. "All right. I need you two to read and sign these papers, which basically say that if you are deemed unfit, the child will return back here, and depending on how unfit, you could have a fine or possible jail time. I don't think that will happen. I have read your home study evaluation, and you two seem perfect."

"Thank you," Mrs. Free said as she read over the paperwork.

Twenty minutes later, they were done with all the paperwork and were getting Amber's items together. They consisted of only a nightgown, toothbrush, and the little jewelry box that Aunt Sophie left her for her birthday.

"I totally forgot about this. Oh my goodness, this was a birthday present for Amber. It belonged to her deceased aunt she lived with. The aunt left Amber this jewelry box and got the twins the bears they have."

"Oh, wow. We'll have to put that on her nightstand," Mrs. Free said as she took it and handed it to Mr. Free.

"Is this it?" Mr. Free asked, holding the few items.

"That's it. Congratulations once again. I hope you three have the family that you've always wanted."

"Thank you. I'll go get Amber and we'll be on our way. We will come visit her sisters every so often, when she would like."

"Great. Remember to stop by here so I can tell her bye."

"I will." Mrs. Free went to get Amber as Mr. Free left to put the belongings in the car. Amber said goodbye to her sisters, walked out of the room, and gave Lucy a big hug.

"Amber, do you know why we went back to the orphanage?" Mrs. Free asked when they get back in the car.

"So I could tell Maddie and Em good night?"

"Yes and no." Amber gave her a confused look. "Baby girl, we adopted you. Do you know what that means?"

"You're my new mommy and daddy?" Amber smiled.

"Yes, we are. And your new last name is Free. So you are now Amber Rose Free."

Amber beamed. She was now free, free from trouble and free from running again. She had a new mommy and daddy who loved her so much. "But what about Maddie and Em?" Amber asked with a frown.

"They will have a new mommy and daddy soon too, I'm sure. And we can have so many sleepovers and parties. Don't worry, sweetie. I promise you that everything is going to work out." Mrs. Free smiled at Amber, but even she was worried about what the future would bring.

They went out to eat and then went home, going to bed not long after that.

"Good morning, Amber," Mrs. Free said as Amber walked into the living room the next morning.

"Morning ..." Amber wasn't fully awake yet.

"Want some breakfast? We have eggs, pancakes, cereal ..."

"I'll just have some cereal."

"All right, sweet pea," Mrs. Free said as Amber was eating, "I've got to clean house today, but after that, we can do whatever you'd like. I have work tomorrow, so you'll have to go stay with my mom. I called her earlier, and she'll be over here later today so you can meet her. She's so excited to meet you."

"Your mom? Would that be my new grandma?"

"Yes, she is."

"What about your dad?"

"He said he can't come over today, but he'll be at their house tomorrow, so you'll be able to meet him then."

Amber finished eating and went to her room to play with the new toys her new mom had bought for her.

A few hours later, Mrs. Free was done cleaning, and she and Amber ate lunch and started watching a movie in the living room. "Okay, Amber, we'll watch this movie, and then we have to go to the grocery store."

At the end of the movie, Amber and her new mom went to Super Mart. She'd done most of her grocery shopping when Amber saw a play-yard she loved.

"Amber, maybe for Christmas, you can ask Santa."

"Good idea. I'll ask him to bring Maddie and Em a new mommy and daddy too."

"Do you want to go see them today?"

"No, that's okay."

They finished their shopping, loaded up the car, and went home. Tammy's mother was already there when they got back. They went inside, and Amber introduced herself.

"You're a beautiful young lady," Tammy's mother, Iris, said.

"Thank you," Amber said, happy again to meet a grandmother.

"Are you ready to come play at my house tomorrow? I know your grandpa would love to meet his beautiful granddaughter."

"Yeah! Do you have toys at your house?"

"You'll have to bring some over. We do have a trampoline with a net outside; it was Tammy's when she was younger. Do you like trampolines?"

"I don't know. I never had one." This made Amber a little sad.

Tammy said, "Amber, how about after work tomorrow, I go over there and jump on it with you?"

"That sounds fun!"

Mr. Free came home at that moment. He talked to Iris for a little bit, and then everybody said their goodbyes.

The next day, Tammy woke Amber up at 7:45 so she could get dressed to go see her new grandparents. "Okay, Amber," Tammy said from the hallway, "get dressed and then put all the toys you want to take in this bag." She handed Amber a Super Mart bag.

Amber did as she was told, packing only a few toys though. "Can I leave them at Grandma's house for next time?"

"Sure, sweetie."

Once they were ready, they hugged and kissed Daniel, then got in the car and went to Grandma's.

"Good morning, Amber!" Iris said as she opened the door.

"Good morning."

"All right, I've got to go to work. I should get off around three thirty, so I'll be here around four. Daniel gets off at four, and he'll swing by afterward. Amber has her bag with some toys in it. I know everything will be fine but call me at work if there are any problems."

"Tammy, calm down. We'll be fine—don't worry. Just get to work."

They said their goodbyes, and Iris took Amber inside to meet Arthur, Amber's new grandpa. "Well, hello, sweetie. You must be Amber. Iris and Tammy have told me so much."

"Hi," Amber said, shaking his hand.

"Have you eaten yet?"

"No, but I'm not really hungry right now."

"That's fine, sweetheart. Let me show you Tammy's old room. You can play in there if you want. We also have a TV in there if you'd like to watch it."

The day went by in a blur. Amber had gone to her mom's old room, played, and watched TV for a while. She then went outside, where they still had Tammy's old bike, and she rode that around for an hour or so. Tammy came over when she got off work and jumped on the trampoline with Amber.

Daniel arrived after work, and they all had dinner with Amber's new grandparents. Amber loved her new family, but she couldn't help but think, *I wonder what Maddie and Em are doing.*

CHAPTER 20

MADISON AND EMILY

B ack at the orphanage, Madison and Emily were having fun playing with their friends. The first night Amber left, the twins were sad; they'd never been separated for that long. She came back the next day to see them, and it was as if she never left. Julie had come in and checked on them as the days passed. Amber hadn't visited in two days, and the twins were actually doing quite well, a big surprise to all the teachers.

"Julie …" Madison began during their "session."

"Yes, Maddie?"

"Can we call Amber? I miss her."

"I'm sure you can. Let me go ask Lucy." She got up and walked out of the room and down the hall. "Lucy, Madison has asked if she could call Amber; she misses her."

"Absolutely. I know the twins miss her, but other than that, how are they doing?"

"They're taking the separation pretty well, if I say so myself. They talk about her, sure, but I don't see any real problems with the girls' behavior. I told them that Amber went to a family who loves her so much. I told them she's having so much fun now. They're happy for her."

"Oh, good. I'm so glad," she said as she was scrolling in her phone for Mr. and Mrs. Free's number. "Here it is."

Julie thanked her for the number and went back to the room. "Okay, Maddie, Em, do you want to talk to Amber?"

"Yeah!"

"All right, let's go in the sleeping room so you can hear her."

"Hi, is this Mrs. Free? This is Julie from the orphanage. Her sisters just wanted to talk to her. Thank you." It was a couple of minutes before Amber came on the line.

"Hello?" she said.

"Hi, sweetie! How are you doing?" Julie had been relieved when Amber answered.

"I'm good. I had a lot of fun today, and I went to see my new grandma and grandpa. I like them."

"That's great. Would you like to talk to Maddie and Em?"

"Sure!"

"Okay, hold on. I'll put you on speakerphone."

"Hi, Amber!" the twins said in unison.

"Hi, Maddie! Hi, Em!" Amber was happy to talk to them.

"We miss you," Madison said with a pout.

"I miss you and Em too. I can ask when I can come see you again. I have to make sure Mo … Mrs. Free's off work." Amber didn't want to use the word *mom* around her sisters. Tammy had said the word itself may remind the twins that they don't have a mom or dad … at least not yet.

While Amber was on the phone, Madison, Emily, and Julie heard her asking Mrs. Free when they could go visit.

"Mrs. Free said we can't come until Monday. Four more days."

"Yay!" Madison and Emily cheered.

"I'm about to watch a movie with them and then go take a bath. I'll talk to you later. I love you all."

"We love you too, Amber," Julie said as she hung up. "I'll go let Lucy and Ms. Rose know she'll be here Monday. You two need to go eat dinner—come on."

Once the girls were eating, she went to let the others know that Amber would come Monday. "Perfect," Lucy said after she got the news. "How did the girls react when Amber came on the phone?" she asked.

"I thought they'd be sad, and they were at first, but once Amber said she'd come Monday, their little faces lit up like it was Christmas."

"That's so good to hear. I just hope when it comes their time to get adopted, the new parents will let them have that relationship with Amber."

"You and me both. Well, I'll go tell the girls goodbye and that I will be back Friday to check back in on them."

"Thank you for being here for them."

"Not a problem," she said, turning to go tell the girls goodbye.

The days leading up to Monday basically went the same as every other day; they ate breakfast, went to play in their rooms until around ten, went outside for a little bit, ate lunch, and played until dinner. They usually had "school," but Ms. Rose thought they should have a couple of weeks' break.

Julie came in on Friday, but the girls were happy and playing, so Julie said she wasn't needed and left, saying she'd be back Monday to see Amber.

The girls had a good weekend playing with their friends, and before they knew it, it was Monday. They woke up with big smiles on their faces when they realized what day it was. They went about their normal routine, and Amber showed up while they were outside.

"Amber!" Madison and Emily shouted, running over to her and almost knocking her over.

"Maddie! Em!" Amber shouted back. She gave her sisters a big hug.

The girls went over to play while Tammy said hello to Ms. Rose and went to tell Lucy they were there.

"Hey, Lucy." Tammy walked into her office.

"Hello, Mrs. Free. How are things? Good, I hope."

"Couldn't be better. Amber has been staying with my parents while I've been at work, and they say she's been perfect, that they couldn't ask for a better granddaughter. She stayed with my husband yesterday, and he told me they bonded."

"That's great. Is she showing any signs of separation anxiety or depression? That's Julie's and my biggest concern regarding these girls." As if on cue, Julie entered the office.

"Hello, Mrs. Free! She beamed when she saw her. "How's everything going?"

"Hi, Julie. Everything is exceptionally well."

"That's good. Is Amber outside with her sisters?"

"She is."

Lucy spoke up. "Julie, before you go see her, can you come sit for just a minute? I actually was just asking Mrs. Free if Amber was having any problems at home."

Julie nodded, shut the door behind her, and took a seat by Tammy. "Mrs. Free, has Amber been having separation problems or any signs of depression? Any of that?"

"No. She's just a perfectly happy little girl. So full of life. On Saturday, she was ready to see her sisters, but she didn't seem depressed or anything. She knew we were coming today, so I think that eased her mind. She knows that on the days I'm off work, she's more than welcome to come up here if she wants to. I'll actually give you my parents' number in case her sisters want to talk to her while she's over there." Julie handed her paper and a pen, and Tammy wrote down her parents' contact information. "You have my husband's number, right?"

"Yes, I do."

"All right, here you go." Tammy gave her the piece of paper.

"Well, it seems Amber's doing just fine, so I'll let you two go outside and see them," Lucy said as they all stood to shake hands. "Thank you for taking care of our Amber," she said to Tammy.

"I think she's taking care of my husband and me." They all laughed. Julie and Tammy went outside to watch the sisters play.

It was soon approaching lunchtime, and Amber was ready to go. "Okay, Amber, say bye to your sisters. Tell them they can call whenever they want."

The next few months were much the same way, the only difference being that instead of going to her grandma and grandpa's, Amber went to school while her parents were at work. Her mom would try to get off work when Amber finished school, but her grandma would have to get her much of the time, not that either of them minded.

Amber went to see her sisters during the weekends for a couple of hours and called them three to four times a week. They were all adjusting well despite being separated.

CHAPTER 21
ADOPTION

"**A**mber, are you ready to go? Where's your basket?" Tammy asked as she went into Amber's room. It was Halloween, and they were all getting ready to go to the Halloween carnival. Amber was dressed as Tinkerbell, Tammy was Wendy, and Daniel was Peter Pan.

"I'm ready!" Amber exclaimed as she grabbed her basket.

Daniel smiled when he saw her. "You look beautiful, little fairy!"

"Thank you, Peter Pan." Amber laughed. "All right, let's go so we can get all the candy."

Their plan for today was to go to the Halloween carnival early, spend a few hours playing games, and then take Amber to see her sisters.

At the carnival, people were already playing games and getting candy. "Okay, Amber, what first?" Tammy asked after they got their tickets.

Amber looked around for a bit until she saw what she wanted to do first. They had fun for a few hours, until Daniel announced that it was time to go.

"Where are we going?" Amber asked when she got in the car.

"We're going to go visit the orphanage, Amber. We have a big bag of candy in the back," Tammy explained.

"For Maddie and Em?"

"Well, it's not all for them, but yes, they can have some."

When they got to the orphanage, Tammy and Amber went inside while Daniel was getting the candy out of the back. "Hi, Lucy," Amber said, stepping behind her desk to give her a hug.

"Hi, Amber." Lucy smiled and hugged her back.

"Happy Halloween!"

"To you too, dear. I love your costume. Are you supposed to be ... Tinkerbell?"

Amber's eyes lit up when Lucy guessed right. "Yeah, and we brought candy! For Maddie and Em too. I'll go tell them." Excited, Amber went to see her sisters.

"Hello, Mrs. Free, good to see you again." Lucy looked up at her.

"You as well. As Amber said, my husband and brought a big bag of candy for all the children and teachers. I'll let you sort it out." Daniel entered the room and placed the candy on her desk.

"Oh, wow, thank you. This is such a surprise; you didn't have to buy this."

"We know. We wanted to. This place has been a big part of Amber's life, even though she was just here for a few months." Tammy smiled. She was such a warmhearted person. Of course, Lucy knew that when she and her husband adopted Amber.

"Amber!" Madison and Emily screamed when Amber walked in.

"Maddie! Em!"

They all gave big hugs, and Ms. Rose walked up to greet

Amber. "Hey, sweetheart, how are you?" she asked, giving Amber a hug.

"I'm good. We brought candy!" Amber had a grin from ear to ear.

"How sweet of you. Are you going trick-or-treating tonight? I love your costume. Are you a fairy?"

"We already got candy. I'm Tinkerbell. Mom is Wendy, and Dad is Peter Pan."

Ms. Rose looked shocked as to how Amber referred to Mr. and Mrs. Free. They were her parents now, but she'd thought it would take longer for her to call them Mom and Dad. "That's fantastic. I love that idea. So cute." As she said that, Tammy and Daniel walked in with a bucket of candy.

"Hello, Ms. Rose." They greeted her with warm smiles.

"Hi, Mr. and Mrs. Free. I love your costumes; it's such a sweet idea."

"Thank you, but I think Amber's love of Peter Pan has to do with this," Daniel said, looking at Amber. They all started laughing. "Well, here's some candy for you and the children. We had Lucy divide it up."

"Awesome! We'll have some after dinner. Thank you so much." She took the candy and went to put it high enough so the kids wouldn't get it. They stayed another few hours, until it was time for the twins to get ready for dinner.

"Are you tired now, Amber?" Tammy asked when they got home.

"Yes," Amber replied with a yawn.

"Come on. You can go to bed now and bathe in the morning. I'm off work, so we can spend the day together."

"Yay." Amber tried to sound excited, but it came out sleepily. She said good night to Daniel and followed Tammy to her room.

"Good night, sweetie," Tammy said as she tucked her in and kissed her forehead.

"Good night, Mommy," Amber said, already half-asleep.

Tammy went into the living room, where Daniel was turning on the TV. "Oh my God, Daniel." Tammy started crying.

"What happened? Is Amber okay?" He looked concerned and worried as he jumped to his feet.

"She's fine, fast asleep. She called me ... Mommy." Tammy went over and cried tears of joy on Daniel's shirt when they sat back down.

"That's awesome! As I told you, we needed to take baby steps. It can't be easy for her."

"I know. I'll try not to make it such a big deal." She stopped crying, and they watched TV before going to bed.

The next morning, Amber woke up and took a bath. When she got out, she went into the kitchen with her hairbrush to find Tammy at the stove.

"Good morning, baby girl," Tammy said when she saw her.

"Good morning. What are you making?"

"Pancakes. We can eat up and go do some grocery shopping. Give me, like, fifteen minutes."

"Okay." Amber went into the living room to watch some cartoons.

They ate breakfast and did all their shopping in two hours. When they returned home, Tammy made Amber lunch and then told her to go play while she put the stuff away. Before they knew it, Daniel got home, and they all spent some time together before having dinner.

Weeks later, it was Thanksgiving break and Amber went to see her sisters again. They had fun for a few hours, until Amber had to leave.

A few new couples had come and gone after Amber had left months ago, but they weren't interested in twins. Lucy was getting worried about them. Would they ever get adopted? And more importantly, would they stay together?

The first week of December, a young couple named Kathryn and Mason Hyde came into the orphanage, saying they wanted to adopt a child by Christmas. Kathryn had beautiful long black hair with blonde tips. She was tall—five feet eight—and worked as a bank teller; Mason was six feet tall and had brown hair. He was an attorney.

"Hello. Mr. and Mrs. Hyde, correct?" Lucy asked, standing as the Hydes entered her office.

"Yes." Mr. Hyde reached out to shake her hand.

Lucy smiled and sat back down as the Hydes were seated. "I already ran background checks, and you two are good to go. So I guess the question is, What ages would you prefer?"

"We'd like to see children between the ages of three and seven," Kathryn said. "I think those are good ages to start."

"All right, let me look real quick." She turned to her computer. "We have five three-year olds, three who are five, four who are six, and two who are seven. We have the rooms split, but I will be more than happy to show you to their rooms."

They headed down the hall to the younger kids' room. Mr. and Mrs. Hyde walked out twenty-five minutes later, in awe of all the kids. Lucy then showed them to the older children's room. They came out after a short while, their minds set on a particular set of siblings.

"How were the children? Good, I hope," Lucy said as they entered her office.

"They were great, so smart and kind," Mrs. Hyde said as they sat.

"Good. I'm glad to hear it. Did you bond with any of them?"

"The twins in the older room. Ms. Rose told me they have an older sister who was adopted. Is that right?"

"Our Madison and Emily. Yes. It's sad when siblings aren't always adopted out together, but Amber is so much happier where she is now and the twins understand that. She and her parents do come visit from time to time."

"That's good to hear," Mr. Hyde said. "We love all the other children, and I don't know these girls' story, but I don't imagine it's good. Am I correct?"

Lucy sighed. "Their story is pretty upsetting. I will tell the story if you do wish to adopt these girls. However, I will need to call someone else in who knows more about them and their emotions. They have had to have some type of therapy that apparently worked wonders."

"Oh, wow. I knew they had to have a history but never imagined them having to have therapy. Were they abused?"

"Physically, no, not that I've heard. They have had some type of abuse, but I don't really know how to classify it."

"Oh … wow." Mrs. Hyde looked both surprised and sad for the girls.

"I do have someone who has been with the girls since all this first started. It's the sheriff in the next town over. I'm not sure of his schedule, but I can call him if you'd like. I can also call the therapist. If you do agree to take them, she may have tips on how to keep them from severe separation anxiety. With Amber, her parents took her for a night, brought her back for about half a day, and took her again. It's a process. The therapist has told me that since the twins are three years younger than their sister, they probably won't remember as much."

"Do they ever have nightmares regarding their past?" Mr. Hyde asked.

"When they first arrived, they all had sleepless nights, but their sister, Amber, had it worse because she is the oldest and remembered the most. She would often wake up in a cold sweat. From what the sheriff told me, Amber was more of a mother figure than a sister to the twins. It's really sad. But now Amber can just be a normal happy eight-year-old, and that's all we want for all these children."

"Of course. If we do plan on taking the twins, will we be able to contact Amber's parents and get them together?" Mrs. Hyde asked.

"Yes. I have all her contact information, and she is definitely willing to keep them together. She gave me total consent to give out this information, if you wish to have it."

"Would we be able to take the twins for the night and see how it works? I'll call Amber's parents personally and let them know we are planning to adopt them."

"Sure. So you have your minds made up?"

"I believe so." She looked at her husband, and he smiled and nodded.

"Okay. Can you wait here about forty minutes so I can try to get the sheriff and the therapist in here? They can hopefully give a little more information about them."

"Certainly. We have nothing else better to do."

"All right, just one second." She got her phone and called Sheriff Ziree and Julie. "They'll be here in about thirty minutes. You two can wait here if you like."

"Thank you." She and her husband started babbling back and forth.

Julie entered the room forty-five minutes later. "Sorry I'm late. Traffic."

"Oh, you're just fine," Lucy said as she and the Hydes stood.

"Julie, this is Mr. and Mrs. Hyde. They're interested in our wonderful twins."

"Hello," Mr. and Mrs. Hyde said as each they shook her hand.

"Have you called Sheriff Ziree?" Julie asked Lucy.

"I have. He should be here soon as well. We went through this once already with Amber, so now I have to ask how the twins will cope—as far as their having to move again."

"Since you are wanting to adopt both of them, they shouldn't have too much of a problem. Amber surprised all of us when she willingly left with her new parents. So I think with the twins, seeing that and knowing that she's happy, healthy, and safe, it helped ease their minds a little and they may just go. Do you two live in the same town as Amber's parents? Naturally, they'll want to meet you and keep Amber and her sisters in contact. Amber now lives in Platte City with her parents."

"No way! That's where we just moved. That's so crazy." Mrs. Hyde laughed and shook her head.

"Wow. Well, here's their address. Maybe you've driven by there?" Lucy handed her a piece of paper.

"Oh my gosh, this is literally right down the road." Mrs. Hyde was happy that she would be able to keep the sisters connected.

"What are the odds? That's wonderful!" Lucy was thrilled.

Sheriff Ziree arrived and had a talk with the Hydes about what all three of the girls had gone through. They all talked for another forty-five minutes before the Hydes were ready to take the girls. Sheriff Ziree and Julie went to get them, and he brought them back to the office while she was letting Ms. Rose know what was happening.

"I hope they do get adopted. They deserve it. And to get

adopted together? That's the best news yet." Ms. Rose was very pleased.

"From the way the Hydes were talking, they really want them." Julie sounded hopeful.

Back in the office, the twins were introduced to the Hydes, and they decided to go have a sleepover with them. They quickly hugged Sheriff Ziree and Lucy and then went back to hug Julie and Ms. Rose as they left. Lucy walked back to her office and called Mrs. Free.

"This is going to be so much fun, girls. We can stay up late, watch TV, and eat candy." Mrs. Hyde was excited.

"Yay!" the twins said.

They drove home, talking and singing most of the way there. When they pulled up, Madison and Emily gasped at the large house in front of them. "Girls, would you two like to live here?" Mrs. Hyde asked.

Madison and Emily jumped up and down, smiling from ear to ear, exclaiming, "Yes!"

"Great. Let me show you around." They all went inside. "This is the living room, the dining room, and the kitchen right over there. In here is a half bath, and we have two upstairs."

Mrs. Hyde led them up the stairs. "And here we have three bedrooms and two bathrooms. I'll let you each pick your own room. Here's the first one …" She opened the door to reveal a medium-sized room with a neatly made bed in the center, a dresser and TV opposite it.

Emily walked in and looked around, determined that this was going to be her room. "We can buy decorations later." Mrs. Hyde smiled at her.

"Okay, Madison, here's your room." She opened another door and revealed a room a little bigger than the other one but having the same things. "And in here is our room, so if you ever need anything during the night or anything, you can always knock on it. It usually stays shut.

"Your bathroom is right over here. There are towels and washcloths. I also bought a few different shampoos and soaps; I didn't know what you two would like. You're more than welcome to take baths or showers tonight. Are you two hungry?"

Madison and Emily nodded.

"All right, let's go get something to eat." They went downstairs to the kitchen, and Mrs. Hyde made them all PB&Js.

CHAPTER 22
FAMILY REUNION

L ater the next morning, Mrs. Hyde received a call from Lucy. "Oh, that's wonderful. The girls will absolutely love that! Tell her it's a definite yes, and you are more than welcome to give her my number. I'm off today, so it would be amazing if we could get together." Mrs. Hyde was smiling big on the phone, and the girls looked at her as if she were crazy.

"Great! I'll call Mrs. Free back and let her know. I hope everything's going well with the twins. Are they adjusting fine?" Lucy asked, hoping they were.

"They're perfect. I gave them a tour of the house last night. They took baths, and we're all playing this morning."

"I'm so glad to hear that. Let me call Mrs. Free and hopefully you can get together."

"All right, thank you."

Mrs. Hyde and the girls played for another thirty minutes, and then she got a text.

"Hi, is this Mrs. Hyde? This is Tammy Free. I'm so happy that you want to keep these girls connected! What is a good time for us to meet?"

"Hi, Mrs. Free. I would hate to separate these girls; they're so sweet. I'm sure they can't wait to see their sister, and I can't wait to meet her. Anytime today would be perfect."

"Amber and I are out right now, and we're about to go eat lunch with my husband. Is 2:00 okay? And your house or mine? I would say the park, but it's way too cold—LOL."

"Two o'clock is perfect. And yes, it's much too cold. We have a swing set, but we told the girls they can't play on it today. They don't have very good coats; I need to go buy them some. Do you think you'd be able to come to my house and watch them for a few minutes while I go get some? I hate having them cooped up in the house."

"Oh, for sure. What's your address?"

"1845 Wilkerson St."

"Our address is 22 Hill Dr. I can't believe how close we are!"

"Wow, that's awesome! So I guess I'll see you at 2:00? I have to go start on lunch for these girls."

"See you at 2:00."

Mrs. Free sent a photo of Amber smiling big. Mrs. Hyde chuckled to herself.

"Okay, girls, it's noon. What do you want for lunch? We can have sandwiches again or I can make hot dogs."

"Hot dogs!" the girls nearly shouted.

"Okay, okay. I guess you girls love hot dogs. Do you want macaroni and cheese too?"

Madison and Emily nodded their heads.

She started boiling water and then got drinks. "Do you two like ketchup, mustard, or relish on yours?" she asked when it was time to fix their plates.

"I like ketchup and mustard," Madison said.

"Ew … ketchup." Emily made a face. "I like mustard and relish."

"All right, here you go. After you two eat, I need you to go wash your hands and faces; we're going to have a visitor later."

At 2:10, the doorbell rang. Mrs. Hyde called for the girls, who were playing in the living room. "Girls, there's someone here to see you." She opened the door and was greeted by a smiling (and freezing) Mrs. Free.

"Come on in. It's horrible out there today."

Once the sisters saw each other, they completely forgot about their moms and went in the other room to play.

"Well then."

Mrs. Free laughed. "Sorry. Amber did that at the orphanage too."

"No problem. They missed each other. I'm sure I'll get to formally meet her."

"It's nice to officially meet you. I'm Tammy." She shook Mrs. Hyde's hand.

"I'm Kathryn. I'm sure we'll be seeing a lot more of each other." They both laughed.

"I'm sure we will. This is a beautiful home, by the way."

"Thank you. We try to keep it nice, although I'm sure now it won't be, but that's totally fine. Shall we go see what the girls are up to?"

They went into the living room, where Amber and her sisters were talking nonstop. "Amber," Tammy said, "come meet Mrs. Hyde. She's going to adopt your sisters."

"Hi," Amber said with a big smile, hugging Mrs. Hyde. "Thank you for adopting my sisters!"

"Hello, sweetie. You're so very welcome. I love your sisters so much already. And I have a feeling we'll get close too." She winked at Amber.

"Yeah! We'll come over every day. Can we?" she asked.

"Honey, I have work most days. We can come as often as

I can. Or if Mrs. Hyde is off work, she could come visit you at Grandma's."

"Oh, okay. Or maybe she could watch me on her days off? Could you, Mrs. Hyde?"

Tammy looked at Kathryn apologetically.

"Sure, Amber. Your mom ... uh ... Mrs. Free would just have to let me know when."

"Yay!"

"Thank you," Tammy said. "She calls me Mom now, by the way." Tammy smiled.

"That's wonderful!" Kathryn said as Amber resumed playing. They played until it was dark out. Daniel had gotten off work and headed over to see them, bringing pizza.

"I'm sorry my husband's working late. I'm sure you two will meet him soon though," Kathryn said.

"That's all right. Well, it's getting late. We should head out. Amber, say bye to your sisters," Tammy said.

"Aw, man." Amber hugged her sisters one by one and walked to the front door to put her jacket on.

"This was great. I had fun, and I know Amber did too. I'll text you when I'm off and maybe we can get together again."

"I'll do the same." Tammy smiled and opened the front door for them.

"Bye, Mrs. Hyde. Bye, Maddie and Em! See you soon!" Amber yelled as they walked out the door.

CHAPTER 23

MORE SURPRISES

t was now August, and the girls and their mothers were all
back-to-school shopping together. January through July had
gone well. When Tammy was working, Amber either went
to school, went to her grandparents' home, or went to visit her
sisters. The twins had essentially the same schedule, and they
would go see Amber when they could. During the summer,
Amber and her sisters practically lived at each other's houses.
Their parents became fast friends and loved getting together
when they could. They were one big happy family.

"Maddie, do you have the highlighters?" her mom asked.

"Here, Mommy," Madison tossed them in the cart.

"Thank you. Emily, pencils?"

"Here, Mommy." Emily threw them in as well.

The girls walked around talking and getting school supplies.
Then it was time for new clothes.

"Yes! I love new clothes and shoes!" Amber was super
excited.

"Calm down, hot stuff. We're just getting you two outfits.
You already have enough clothes to last a month without
washing." Tammy laughed, but she wasn't kidding.

"Let's look over here!" Amber took Maddie and Em to a section with cute clothes; their mothers followed.

"Hey, can you watch Amber?" Tammy asked. "I have to go to the bathroom."

"Sure. We'll be here." Kathryn watched the girls going through the clothes.

"Thanks."

As Tammy walked to the bathroom, she felt nauseated. She just blew it off. *Maybe I just had a bad lunch. Or maybe I need some water.*

When Tammy came back, she and Amber went into a dressing room so Amber could try on the new clothes; Tammy and the other two went into another.

"Perfect fit!" Tammy was happy with the clothes Amber had chosen. "So that's one outfit and shirt. Let's go find more pants." As Tammy and Amber went out to find more, Kathryn was struggling with the twins.

"Hey, Kat, need help?" Tammy asked through the door.

"If you can fit it here, I'd love some help. These girls just don't want to try on clothes." They were in the big handicap stall, which was large enough to accommodate all of them.

"What's wrong, girls?" Tammy asked when she got in there.

"We don't want to try on clothes," Emily whined.

"I know you don't, but look, Amber tried on some already; we just need one more pair of pants."

"Yeah!" Amber accidentally used her outside voice. Tammy frowned at her. "Sorry, Mom. Em, it's not so bad. Here, we'll do it together." Amber helped Emily into a shirt. "See, perfect. One shirt down." Amber smiled at their accomplishment.

"Okay, Amber. How many more, Mommy?" Emily asked her mom.

"Two more. You and Maddie have to get three outfits each."

169

Maddie heard the conversations and decided to try on clothes too.

"Amber, let's get your last pair of pants and leave; I don't feel too well," Tammy told Amber.

"Okay, Mom." Amber and her mom left the dressing room, and Amber ran to find more pants.

"Tam, you all right?" Kathryn asked when she and the twins emerged from the dressing room.

"I'm just a little light-headed and nauseous. I'm sure it's just a bug," Tammy said, but she wasn't so sure.

"Could you be pregnant?"

"What? No. Daniel and I have stopped trying, and I'm on the pill. We're perfectly happy with our little family."

"Tam, the pill doesn't always work, and bringing a baby into the world now would just mean a bigger family to love it. Just take a test, all right?"

"Okay."

By the time they went home, the girls had shopped for school, gotten their hair cut, and played at the park. Tammy had gone home after Amber got her hair cut, and Amber was staying the night with her sisters.

"Let me know first thing after you take the test," Kathryn said in a text to Tammy.

"I will. I'll test first thing in the morning, before heading to work."

What if we did add a baby to the mix? Tammy wondered. *There's no doubt that Amber would be a great sister—she already is one—but what about me? I don't have any experience with babies. I'm working myself up; there's no way I'm pregnant.*

Daniel had come home, and Tammy told him about her day and the possibility of her being pregnant, saying she was taking a pregnancy test in the morning.

"That's great!" Daniel was thrilled. "Honey, we love Amber as if she were our own, but we've always wanted our own. The timing is perfect. You have me, Mason, Kathryn, Amber, and the twins to help with anything and everything."

"But what if I have Amber and her sisters plus a baby over here? That's four kids; I can barely handle the three."

"It's not going to be easy; we know this. Just take the test in the morning and ease all our minds. If we are pregnant, we'll talk more about it; and if we're not, I'll be a little disappointed, but we'll be fine. I promise. Let's shower and watch some TV."

The next morning, Tammy crawled out of bed and went into the bathroom to get ready for work.

"You're going to take this, right?" Daniel asked, standing in the doorway, holding the test kit. Tammy was already in the bathroom washing her face.

"Holy shit, Daniel!" Tammy screeched. "You scared me! I forgot you go in later today." Tammy snatched the test from him. "Okay, okay. Go wait on the bed or something." She shooed him out and shut the door behind him.

A few minutes later, she emerged. "I'm not pregnant. We were worried for nothing." Tammy was smiling and trying to hold back tears, but Daniel heard the sadness in her voice.

"Come here." Daniel had his arms open for her. "Now we know. I want a baby, but I'm so happy we have Amber—and her sisters, when we all get together or they come spend the night. Let's just get ready for work so we can put this behind us."

They both got ready for work, and Tammy left a little before Daniel. He was going to drop Amber off to stay with Kathryn.

"Hey, I took the test," Tammy texted Kathryn a bit later that morning. "It was negative. I'm at work now. Tell Amber I love her and will see her after."

"I'm sorry, girl," Kathryn texted back a few minutes later.

"If you need me, I'm here. Amber said she loves you too."
Kathryn sent a picture of Amber looking as if she had just
woken up.

"Thanks, Kat. That made me feel better." She sent the text
with a heart emoji.

Tammy went back to work. When she finished her shift and
was driving to Kathryn's, her vision went blurry and she lost
control of her car. Thankfully, there were a few cars behind her,
and the drivers all ran to her aid.

"Hello, miss. Are you all right?" one man asked.

"Hello," Tammy said weakly.

"You're going to be okay. The ambulance is coming. I'll
stay right here. Do you want me to call someone? Husband …
mother?"

"Daniel. Amb—" was all that came out before she was
unconscious.

Tammy woke up in a white room and forgot that she had
wrecked her car. Had it not had been for the pain in her leg,
she'd have thought she was dreaming.

"Baby, I was so worried." Daniel jumped up and hugged
her. "Are you okay? What happened?"

"I … don't know. I got off work and was going to get Amber.
Amber! Is she okay? Did you call Kat?"

"I called her, and they're on their way, Mason too; your
parents are also coming. Don't worry. Please just relax."

"Oh, you're awake. I'm Ms. Stride, your nurse. How are
you feeling?"

"My leg hurts a little, but other than that, I feel fine."

"Well, I can't issue pain meds just yet. Are you her
husband?" Ms. Stride asked Daniel.

"Yes, I am."

"I'll need to go get the hospital paperwork for you to fill out.

I first need to ask you some questions. Is it okay if he stays?" Ms. Stride asked Tammy, who nodded her head.

"Do you remember anything that happened?"

"Yes. I got off work and was driving to pick up my daughter."

"Do you remember feeling dizzy at any point?"

"No."

Ms. Stride was reading the paperwork. "Any medications or drugs? Do you smoke or drink?"

"No ... and no to both."

"Okay. Is there a chance you might be pregnant?"

"I took two tests this morning, and they were both negative."

"Oh, sorry to hear that. I'm going to take some blood, if that's all right, and we're just going to check to make sure everything's okay."

"All right, there we go." Ms. Stride said after she finished a few minutes later. "I'll get this to the lab and bring back those papers for you to fill out," she told Daniel.

"Thank you," Daniel said.

"Daddy!" Amber ran into the room and hugged Daniel as he was trying to finish the paperwork.

"Amber, hi!" Daniel was relieved to see her.

"Mommy, are you all right?" Amber looked over at Tammy.

"I'm fine, baby. Thank you." she looked up at a concerned Kathryn.

"What happened?" Kathryn asked, going over to hug Tammy.

"All I remember is that I was on my way to get Amber and my car flipped and I passed out."

"Thank goodness someone saw it and called it in."

"Yeah. Where are the twins?"

"In the waiting room with Mason and your parents. They didn't want to overcrowd the room."

"Oh, okay."

An hour of chitchat (and people rotating) later, Tammy decided to take a small nap, so everyone went out into the waiting room.

"Mr. Free," Dr. Newman called out a while later.

"Yes? Is my wife all right?" Daniel walked over to him, with Tammy's parents close behind.

"Oh, yes, she'll be absolutely fine. Her iron was extremely low, but we gave her some. That's what she passed out from. I think she got extremely dizzy and lost control of her car. She doesn't really remember because she was also fading in and out of consciousness. She keeps complaining about her legs. When she flipped the car, one of her keys somehow managed to fly off the keychain and landed in her leg, but thank goodness it was just her leg. We got the key out when she first arrived. There is a little medicine in her bag to help with the pain. She'll need to stay overnight."

"How the hell did a key do that? Anyway, I'll have to get my daughter and me home, but I'll be back first thing tomorrow. Is there anything else?"

"Yes. She told our nurse that she had taken two pregnancy tests."

"Yes, I was with her."

"Well, according to her blood work, she *is* pregnant. She's just early on, which is why it didn't show up with the home tests yet. Congratulations."

"*Really?* Oh my God, this is amazing! Thank you so much, Doctor!" Tammy's parents overheard, gave him a hug, and congratulated him.

"Can I go see her?" he asked.

"She's still sleeping and needs to recover. Plus, she doesn't know that part yet. You're more than welcome to come back in the morning. We will have to tell her when she wakes up."

"That's fine. This is just so amazing. We will be back first thing in the morning. Thank you so much."

"My pleasure. See you tomorrow."

"We have to get home, but we will also come back tomorrow. We are so excited that Tammy is pregnant!" Tammy's mom said as they were walking back to the rest of the group.

"Not as excited as I am!" Daniel chuckled. "Amber, come give your grandma and grandpa a hug. We'll see them tomorrow when we come back."

"Bye, everybody!" Iris said. "And congratulations, Daniel."

Daniel told everyone else what was going on.

"*Pregnant?*" Kathryn was surprised and excited.

"I had the same reaction." Daniel was elated.

"I saw you speaking loudly over there, but I didn't hear what it was about. Congratulations! That's so wonderful! I was wondering why Tammy's mom congratulated you." Kathryn hugged him.

"Congrats, man. I know you two have wanted your own." Mason shook his hand and hugged him.

"What do you think, Amber? Do you want another little sister or a little brother this time?" Kathryn asked.

"A brother." Amber smiled.

"Well, we'll see later on. Tammy has to stay overnight, but I'm going to head home with Amber. We'll come back first thing tomorrow."

Eight months later …

"Daniel, Daniel, wake up. I think my water broke." Tammy shook Daniel awake.

"What? Oh, okay." It was five in the morning, but as soon

as Daniel realized what Tammy had said, he shot up. "You go try to wake Amber. I'll get the bags."

"Amber, honey." Tammy turned on the light. "It's time."

Amber groaned in her sleep but got up a minute later. "Time for what?" she mumbled as she got dressed.

"Time to go to the hospital!" Tammy said.

"Oh, yay!" Amber began to pick up speed while dressing.

Daniel showed up in the doorway. "Come on, you two. The car's all packed and ready to go." They all got in the car and headed to the hospital, calling their friends and family on the way.

Daniel also called the hospital before they got there. "Hi, I'm Daniel Free, and my wife is Tammy Free. She's in labor. Is her doctor in?"

"Not yet, but we will call and make sure he gets here."

"All right, thanks. We'll be there in a few minutes."

"Yes, sir. We'll be waiting."

When they got there, a staff member was waiting with a wheelchair to wheel her back. "Hello! Are you excited?" one of the nurses asked Amber.

"Yeah!" Amber said.

"We're just leaving. Give us twenty minutes. Which room?" Kathryn texted Daniel.

"Great. Room 305."

Kathryn, Mason, the twins, and Tammy's parents arrived within a half hour.

"Great to see you again. Hi, girls," Iris greeted them.

"Hi!" the twins said in unison.

"This is so exciting," Kathryn said.

"It is! My baby's having a baby; it's a little emotional too," Iris said.

"Hey, guys." Daniel walked into the lobby, and Amber ran to her sisters.

"Daniel!" Iris greeted, squeezing him. "I'm so excited. Hi, Amber! Are you excited, sweetie? She does want me in the delivery room, right? Oh, I have to go see her."

"Calm down, Grandma," Daniel chuckled. "Yes, she wants you in the delivery room. Hey, can you watch Amber while I go in there also?" he asked Kathryn.

"Why is that even a question? You just go make sure my best friend and your baby are okay."

"Thanks. Amber, stay with Kathryn. We're going to go check on Mom and hopefully have the baby soon."

"Okay!" Amber said excitedly.

Two Hours Later

"Oh my God, perfection!" Iris said as soon as she saw the new baby. The nurses then took the baby to clean him, and Daniel and Tammy's mom left to let Tammy rest a few minutes.

"We'll be right back. We're going to go tell everyone the baby made it."

"All right," Tammy said.

"The baby's here!" Daniel announced when they walked into the lobby. "But we ask that everybody waits, like, fifteen minutes or so. Amber, come on. Come meet the new baby. Here, sanitize first." Daniel and Amber walked toward the room while everyone else waited in the lobby.

"Amber, come here," Tammy said as the nurses handed her the baby. "We'd like you to meet your new brother, Ayden James."

"Hi, Ayden! I'm your sister, Amber. We're going to be best friends!" Amber was so excited to be a big sister again, and she loved him so much already.